BITTERSWEET MOTIVES

Serena Manchester Mysteries,
Book #2

TYORA MOODY

Tymm Publishing LLC
Columbia, SC

Bittersweet Motives
Serena Manchester Mysteries, Book 1

Copyright © 2019 by Tyora Moody

Paperback ISBN: 978-1-7336967-2-2
Ebook ISBN: 978-1-7336967-3-9

Published by:
Tymm Publishing LLC
701 Gervais Street, Suite 150-185
Columbia, SC 29201
www.tymmpublishing.com

Editing: Felicia Murrell
Cover Design: TywebbinCreations.com

Dedication

This book is dedicated to every reader who has reached out to me in the last four years asking for the next Serena book. Your encouragement means the world to me.

Acknowledgements

It's finally here! I pitched this book a few years ago to my then publishing company. My heart was broken when the imprint dismantled. Despite the delays, I want to give a shout out to Joylynn Ross who encouraged my evolution as a writer with the Victory Gospel Series, where Serena Manchester was first introduced as an investigative reporter. I knew by the time I finished the Victory Gospel Series, that Serena was a character who needed her own books. Later, Joylynn helped with the editing of the spin-off book, Hostile Eyewitness.

On the journey with me for the long awaited second book is an editor who has helped shape books in two other book series. Thank you, Felicia Murrell, for your eye for details. I feel that I've grown as a writer.

I often wondered if it was meant for me to ever get back to this series. I had some encouragement along the way on social media from readers like Pastor Rena Anderson. It has always tickled me to see your name, and honestly, I felt led to refer to Serena by her nickname, "Rena" more with this book.

As always, I appreciate readers who take a chance on reading one of my books, especially readers who don't often read mysteries. Thank you in advance for adding *Bittersweet Motives* to your reading list.

Table of Contents

Chapter One

Georgetown, South Carolina

Wednesday, November 7, 7:35 pm

This is really what my life has become. Spying on people.

I peered through my newly acquired Nikon camera, pondering for the third time why I was standing out in the cold. The sunset had occurred well over an hour ago. I was dressed in black from head-to-toe, but I should have dressed warmer. My black bomber jacket seemed useless against the sharp breeze fueled by the Atlantic Ocean. I stood crouched in the shadows of the beach house. The entire back of the house had ocean view windows. I wished I could be on the inside, experiencing the crashing waves I heard behind me.

I never understood why people left windows open for all the world to see. I guess the tall shrubbery around the expensive home provided some sense of security. I huddled in the darkness, not daring to come any closer. I had scoped out the motion detectors and cameras around the house last week, and to keep my cover, I had to remain concealed at least fifty feet away. I hoped that would be enough. I also needed something to happen soon. For freezing my butt off, I needed the satisfaction of finally nailing Edwin Peters in the act this evening.

Alright, Serena. Stay focused. Stop with the complaining.

I quieted my inner whining as the man appeared in my camera lens, and then adjusted the zoom. After talking in depth with the salesman at Best Buy and a few tests, I knew the 70-300 millimeter telephoto zoom lens would capture what I needed from this distance. I felt fairly certain I could deliver images good enough for my employer, Clay Matthews and his client, Mrs. Judith Peters.

In another lifetime, I'd been an investigative reporter at a television station in Charlotte, North Carolina. For over twenty years, I was constantly on the move breaking the latest news stories. For one particular story involving corruption in the city of Charlotte, I pushed too far for the truth and found myself at the bottom of a stairwell, left to die by a madman. Three years had passed, and while I'd recovered from my head injury, I lost my career in the process. I still had days when my old noggin wasn't exactly one hundred percent, but I longed for the days when I investigated more than a man cheating on his wife. Or vice-versa.

I'd followed the Georgetown businessman for a week, hoping to catch him. I was hoping to catch him at his office building, Waterway Commercial Real Estate, but Peters had sense enough to not have the typical young, good-looking secretary. I'd done so many of these cases over the past year with a spouse wanting me to track down their cheating spouse. Often these illicit affairs started at the workplace, and usually the man was with his secretary or a co-worker.

How cliché!

It was fairly common knowledge from my conversations around town, that Edwin had been cheating on his wife for years. Until recently, his wife had either been turning a blind eye or was really that clueless. Judith Peters was a long-time educator and the current principal of McDonald Elementary School. I suspected the woman chose to keep her head in the sand as a way to preserve her privacy. Recently, something had changed or shifted in the marriage to light a fire under Judith. As a result, about a month ago, she filed for divorce. Thankfully, she hired my brother-in-law and current employer to take her case.

Despite Edwin openly sneaking around with other women, the past week seemed a waste of my time. With a pending divorce, maybe Edwin had finally come to his senses. Or, maybe his lawyer warned him about the possibility of someone like me trying to catch him in the act.

Tonight, I'd followed Edwin to Pawleys Island. From piecing together a timeline, I discovered Edwin had officially moved out of the Georgetown family home around the time I started tailing him last week. The man made the trek each day to the family's expensive waterfront property. From my background search on Edwin, he owned the family home and the beach house, with both being in the million dollar price range. A price range that was staggering to me. It also made this assignment of yet another cheating spouse slightly more interesting than past assignments. The divorce between Edwin and Judith, his wife of twenty-two years, was going to be an all out war. My mission was to deliver the arsenal Mrs. Peters needed for her side of the battle.

That isn't going to be a problem tonight.

Twenty minutes into scoping the side of the house, a young woman arrived driving a lime green Volkswagen Beetle. She seemed familiar to me. I'd seen the sandy curly hair recently, but where wasn't coming to me. I creeped, tiptoeing like some cat burglar towards the back of the house. Behind the house, I'd found the perfect spot to see into the kitchen through the glass windows. Edwin had a glass of white wine ready for the young woman as she shrugged out of her coat.

I squatted, feeling my knees protest. Too much time sitting in my car over the past few days made my forty-three year old body my enemy. Age was already a factor, but the lack of physical activity was no fun. And thanks to the cold, crisp November air, a steady weariness had crept into my bones. My fingers had started to stiffen from holding the camera, but quitting wasn't an option. I wiggled around, trying to make my position as comfortable as possible despite the wind at my back, peering through the camera lens again. By the way Edwin's arm was wrapped around the young woman, I'd say in exactly sixty seconds, I would have plenty of provocative photos to share with Mrs. Peters.

Hello! It's about time!

I watched Edwin guide the young woman by the shoulders into another part of the house. I shifted slowly to the right, seeing them appear in another room. I dared to move closer, keeping in mind I needed to stay at least fifty feet from the patio to avoid triggering the motion detectors. Game over for this assignment if I did. I peered easily inside a bedroom. As Edwin slipped the young woman's dress off her shoulder, I positioned the camera lens.

Click. Click. Click.

The young woman's dress fell to the floor displaying her bare backside, and I pulled the camera from my flushed face. I hated this part of the job.

When I joined my brother-in-law's law firm as his private investigator, chasing after adulterous spouses was not what I had in mind. Last year, I'd pushed my way into a police investigation, and while the detectives won't admit it, I solved not one, but two homicide cases for them. Those cases served as the catalyst I needed to push me past the funk I'd been in since my lengthy hospitalization years ago. I had a thirst for seeking the truth and solving criminal cases.

Almost a year later, my fantasy of being the most sought-after private investigator in the state of South Carolina had slowly fizzled to a faded dream. I needed a new kind of case.

I took a deep breath and returned the camera to my eyes.

I cringed. Edwin had his shirt off, and all that chest hair made me want to gag.

Or, maybe the source of my queasiness was the young woman. She had to be young enough to be the

6

man's daughter. Through the camera lens, her bronze complexion was clear. Despite the ruby red lips, she barely seemed eighteen to me.

Something shifted between the two as I watched the young woman's hand slap Edwin across the face. A red mark was visible on his face.

But Edwin's next move made me gasp in shock.

He'd wrapped his hands around the young woman's throat.

Was he trying to kill her or was this something kinky?

Without realizing it, I'd stepped forward from the shadow of my hiding place with my eyes still peeking through the lens. My fingers pressed the camera's button capturing the woman as she flung her hands at Edwin's face again. Her ruby red fingernails made contact with his face, leaving a definitive scratch across his left cheek.

He reached out and slapped the woman causing her to fly backwards out of my line of sight. Edwin moved towards her like a raging bull, his arms outstretched. I could no longer see either of them.

This assignment had gone horribly wrong. Was he going to kill her?

I have to do something.

I shoved the camera in my side bag, crouched down and moved closer to the patio doors outside the bedroom. I certainly didn't want to be responsible for this young woman's death. I also couldn't blow my cover. Mrs. Peters and Clay were counting on me to deliver confidential images.

Screams pierced my ears.

What should I do?

I'd been to the gun range the last few months and finally received a license to carry my SIG. But it wasn't on me and my car was parked down the street.

If I moved any closer, I would risk being caught on the security camera and triggering the motion detector near the patio.

The motion detectors.

I looked around for a way to distract Edwin.

My eyes fell to the tiny pebbles that lined the patio shrubbery. I grabbed a few and, without a second thought, flung one towards the patio.

It was too quiet.

I threw more pebbles, hearing them bouncing off the side of the house.

Edwin appeared at the sliding door, his face a contortion of anger and concern.

I ducked down, but my feet almost slipped in the sand. I scrambled backwards towards the tall shrubbery, hoping the young woman wasn't hurt and could get away.

Edwin slid the door and peered out. His eyes glimpsed in my direction. *Could he see me?* The wind caused the shrubbery to sway around me. I hoped that would keep my hiding spot concealed. My heart was beating in my chest. I'd never been this close to being discovered by my assignment. I'd never been in these conditions either, shivering in the cold with the possibility of a murder or attempted murder taking place right before my eyes.

This was definitely a different kind of assignment.

Not seeing anything, Edwin's face scrunched in fury. Sliding the door closed, he retreated and I used that moment to make my move. I had plenty of photos; I needed to get out of here. Conscious of the security camera, I pulled my baseball cap down towards my head and moved close to the shrubbery until I'd made it around the side. I sprinted towards my car, thankful for the darkness and the quietness of the nearby homes.

Once inside my car, I whipped out my phone and dialed 9-1-1.

"What's your emergency?"

"I'm at 6100 Sunset Lane. A young woman has been assaulted."

The dispatcher responded, "Can you tell us what's happening?"

I huffed into the phone. "You need to get someone here now. I think he's trying to kill her."

If he hasn't already.

The silence after those screams had me anxious and scared.

I was a newbie to my newfound faith and still found praying a bit awkward. But tonight, I stuttered a prayer. *God, please protect that young woman.*

Chapter Two

Wednesday, 8:30 pm

I waited inside my car until I saw a police cruiser arrive in front of the beach house. From where I sat, I could barely see the front of the house. A male police officer climbed out of the City of Pawleys Island Crown Victoria and walked up to the house. I glanced around to see if the police cruiser had attracted any attention from nearby neighbors. The expensive homes were built pretty far apart, but not enough to not notice unusual activity. The police cruiser drove up quietly, no sirens. I imagined that had to do with the address they were tasked to drive to. Money always played a factor.

Before opening my car door, I saw headlights down the road behind me. I waited until the car, which appeared to be a BMW passed me. Whoever was in the car didn't slow to observe the police cruiser, instead they sped up. Once the glow of the taillights faded in the distance, I climbed out of my Honda, pulled my hat down low and sprinted over to nearby trees. I needed to see what was happening.

The palm trees I stood behind weren't thick in the trunk, but combined with the shadows of the house, they provided the cover I needed to glimpse the front door. It seemed like the police officer knocked for a long time before Edwin appeared at the door with a royal blue robe wrapped around his thick body. The former linebacker was probably incredibly handsome thirty years ago. Now, he had a pudgy grandfather look going.

There were no signs of the young woman, though her lime green Beetle remained parked in the driveway. I waited a beat as Edwin let the police officer inside his beach house.

After what seemed like forever, the young woman walked out of the house with the police officer behind her. She wore the same dress, leggings and boots she arrived in, and although her coat was swung around her shoulders, she appeared to be shivering. Probably traumatized. Edwin stood at the door glaring at both of them. I watched as the cop talked to the younger woman who stood with her head low, her eyes shifting from Edwin to her car. Whatever the cop said had the woman dashing towards her car.

The cop returned to the house to talk to Edwin. I decided to follow the young woman. It occurred to me with Edwin's behavior, the girl could be more valuable to Clay on the stand. Did Judith experience Edwin's temper too? Maybe she'd been afraid of him all this time. Most importantly, I wanted to know the girl's name and if she was alright. I couldn't shake the feeling that I'd seen her before.

Who was she?

I returned to my car in time to hear the girl's car engine rev. I quickly cranked my own car and switched the headlights on. Driving past Edwin's beach house, I glanced towards the front door where he stood talking to the cop. He seemed subdued. I hoped my car appeared to be another random car rolling down the street despite the dark, quiet neighborhood.

It wasn't a secret that the businessman and his wife were going through a bitter divorce. Georgetown was a small town. Who knew? Maybe this had happened before with the police showing up at their home.

At the end of the block, I took a left to catch up with the Volkswagen Beetle. The young woman didn't waste any time getting away from Edwin. For her sake, I hoped she decided to press charges and never returned. I tailed the woman at a distance. I had to admit, I was good at this. I had always been good at following people, even from my investigative reporter days. It was how I nailed several stories.

I almost died three years ago trying to nail a story.

I was grateful when we entered back into the city of Georgetown. My bed was calling to me after such a long day, but I had to see this through. Even though following the young woman was way beyond my assignment.

I turned into an apartment complex behind the Beetle and hung back as the young lady swung her car into a parking space. I pulled into a space across from the apartment and switched off the engine. Observing from my rearview mirror, I watched the woman scramble from the car towards an apartment. I opened my car door and closed it softly. I needed to see which apartment she went into. I casually walked down the sidewalk, listening as her feet tapped up the stairs. I drew closer and saw her turn to one of the apartments in the back. Whether right or left, I didn't know.

I looked around and moved towards the stairs, then waited at the bottom to listen. It was really quiet, not even the sounds of a television came from any of the apartments. I reached for my phone in my back pocket and saw it was almost nine o'clock. Someone should be watching whatever primetime show was on right now. I'd rarely watched primetime television and chose to binge-watch Netflix when I wanted some entertainment.

Slowly, I climbed the stairs until I reached the top. I looked around and decided to take another chance, walking quickly to the apartment door on the left marked D6.

I leaned down to listen and then knocked on the door. This was way far out of the assignment, but I needed to find out more about the girl. In my heart, I wanted to see if she was okay. I'd seen enough abused women, especially young women, in my career. On more than one occasion, I had personally experienced a man's hands on me.

A small, female voice answered from the other side. "Who is it?"

Now that I was here, what was I supposed to do?

I decided to go with the truth. Or at least partially.

"Hi, I'm Serena Manchester. I wanted to make sure you were okay."

Silence met me on the other side. Until the voice spoke, "Who are you?"

"I saw Mr. Peters hurting you. I just wanted to make sure you were okay." I waited another second, "I know this is weird and I probably should leave, I just wanted to know if you were okay. I'm walking away now. Stay safe. Stay away from Edwin."

I was halfway to the stairs when the door yanked open. The young woman peeked out from behind the door and glared at me. "Who are you?"

I turned around and walked back slowly. Up close, her eyes were a piercing blue against her deeply tanned face. I reached out my hand. "I'm a private investigator."

She stepped out, shutting the door slightly behind her. The young woman stared at my hand as if I was holding a weapon, and then peered around as if we had spies around us. Her voice was barely above a whisper. "Who sent you?"

I took a tentative step forward, hoping she would let me in. "No one sent me. You're safe, I promise. I just wanted to talk."

She peered around again. That's when I noticed she was shaking. And then I saw the bruising around her throat.

She must have noticed my staring and quickly covered her throat with her hand.

It didn't do much to hide the bruising. "Do you need me to call someone for you?"

She shook her head.

"I saw what he did. Look, if you're afraid..."

Her eyes grew wide. "You can't do anything. I don't know what you want, but please leave me alone."

I swallowed, feeling a lump in my own throat. Her fear was palpable, and I could feel the muscles in my back tense like I needed to run from something myself.

I reached inside my pocket. "If you need to talk to someone or if you need some help, don't hesitate to call me. Mr. Peters is not a good man."

She bit her lip, seeming even younger than I originally thought. For whatever reason, she snatched my business card, slipped inside and slammed the door closed.

I stood for a minute, not sure what to do. Walking back down the stairs, I started to question why I followed the girl. I probably hadn't helped matters and wondered if I made her even more afraid.

I was still new to my relationship with God. His presence in my life was a large reason why I moved from Charlotte and started back over in the place that I'd run away from almost twenty-five years ago. I wasn't sure why, but it felt like my assignment had switched from the disgruntled wife to making sure this young woman was okay. As a P.I., my job was to capture photos of Edwin and return the evidence to Clay. But the former investigative reporter side of me wanted to expose Edwin Peters for more than his indiscretions outside his marriage. For some reason, I sensed his involvement with the young woman could lead to something more.

As I climbed back into my car, I couldn't shake fearing for the young woman. Haunted by her wide eyes and the rawness of the bruises around her neck, I sat for a moment before starting the engine.

Once again, in less than an hour, I found myself praying for the woman's protection.

Lord, is there something more I can do for this young woman? I'm afraid for her. I don't think it was a coincidence that I was at the beach house tonight, but it pains me to see someone so close to death. Please protect her.

***

By the time I arrived home, it was after ten o'clock, and I hadn't had a meal since around noon. I didn't realize how starved I was until I opened my fridge. Thank goodness there were leftovers from my younger sister Beverly Lawson-Matthews, known affectionately to me as Bev. Since relocating from Charlotte back to my home in Georgetown, my relationship with my family had improved. Not only did I work for my brother-in-law, I attended church with my younger sister and her family most Sundays. This was a huge deal for me since I hadn't stepped foot in a church for the majority of years I lived in Charlotte. I grew up a church girl with an overbearing religious stepdad.

Bev loved her dad, Reverend Thomas Lawson. With seven years between us, the center of our disagreements often led to the fact that I despised her dad. My dad, Dallas, chose not to be around except on special occasions. I was mainly raised with Reverend Lawson as the father figure in my life, and from my perspective, the man didn't like my dad and he sure didn't like me. Mama and Bev thought my perspective was all wrong, but I didn't. So I stayed in Charlotte for almost twenty-five years as the estranged family member.

Since returning home, I'd made peace in so many ways. I realized the religious nature of my upbringing drove me from God, when what I needed most was a relationship with God.

It made all the difference for my screwed up mind.

I was no cook, but Bev loved to cook, especially on Sundays, and my sister usually made sure I had a doggie bag of food to bring home with me. Today was Wednesday and I hadn't touched the containers in my fridge, but I was more than ready for the leftover lasagna. As I waited for the microwave to heat up the food, I fed my roommate.

The calico cat slunk into the kitchen from wherever she'd been slumbering for the day. My guess was Callie had made herself comfortable on my bed. I had long since given up on trying to scold the cat since she lived in this house long before me.

I inherited the cat, along with the house, from my Aunt Claudia when she passed away last year. Better known as Aunt C, she was like a second mom to me. Despite my many years living in Charlotte, she decided the way to get me back home was to leave me her house.

It worked.

After satisfying Callie with a plate of Fancy Feast Chunky Chicken, I grabbed my laptop from the living room. My mind remained on the young woman who escaped Edwin Peters' clutches tonight. She still seemed familiar to me. I grabbed the lasagna from the microwave and sat at the kitchen table. While tapping on my laptop, I greedily relished the pasta, beef, tomato and ricotta cheese.

The first place I decided to start was social media, in particular, Edwin Peters' Facebook page. Doing background checks, I have found people post pretty revealing stuff to their social media. It took me fifteen minutes, but I found the girl. I would have missed her if I wasn't looking so hard. She stood in the background of a group of people, her curly hair had been straightened and hung around her face. Interestingly enough, Edwin was in the picture standing next to Mrs. Peters. I checked the time date stamp on the picture.

The photo was taken six months prior to Judith filing for divorce. The Peters appeared to be a happy couple. On one side stood a tall, young woman with dark hair who was the spitting image of Edwin, except a whole lot prettier. I knew the Peters had one daughter and one son. The brunette had to be Janine Peters. On the other side of Judith was a young man who looked like the mini-male version of his mother.

It occurred to me as I stared at Janine and the woman I'd seen tonight that they could be friends. They looked about the same age. I clicked Janine's Facebook profile hoping she kept it public.

As I scrolled down her profile I started to see a pattern. Most of Janine's photos were posted from Instagram. I imagined most women her age hung out on Instagram more. In one click, I found myself scrolling through Janine's photos, and the more I scrolled, the more disturbed I became.

The young woman I saw with Edwin tonight appeared to be a really close friend of his daughter. There were photos of the two women in a variety of places from restaurants, bars and the beach. When I found a photo that was tagged, I clicked and found myself staring at the profile photo of the other woman.

Samantha Livingston's bright smiling face stared back at me from selfie after selfie. She wore skimpy clothes that, even in my more provocative days, I wouldn't dare wear. What really surprised me was the 30,000 plus followers she had on her Instagram profile. She was like a fashion celebrity with many of her posts not only showing off clothes, but hairstyles and makeup ideas.

I shut the laptop and sat back in my kitchen chair. The lasagna in my stomach seemed to flip-flop as I recalled the older man's hands on his daughter's friend. I'd seen and met some pretty sick people in my years, but I couldn't shake the feeling that would probably consume me the rest of the night.

Chapter Three

Thursday, November 8, 7:55 am

I woke up the next morning determined to make it to the office early so I could show the photos to Clay. When I opened my front door, the cold breeze slapped me in the face. Life always had a way of stopping me in my tracks. Today's obstacle made my cheeks burn as my eyes caught sight of the man walking up my driveway.

I sucked in a breath and stepped back as Trey Evans reached the top of my porch steps. His grin was infectious as usual, despite the slight annoyance that rose up in me. It wasn't so much that I didn't enjoy seeing him, it was that my attempts to avoid him seemed to crash and burn.

"Glad I caught you before you headed out for the day." Trey's smile was easy going, but his brown eyes silently pleaded for me not to do what I was thinking.

He knew I wanted to bolt. It had been my pattern for months now. For a split second, I felt trapped. I hadn't done anything strenuous, but suddenly I felt like I couldn't breathe. I stepped back towards the door as if I needed it to hold me up.

Trey didn't move towards me.

He knew me.

His voice drifted softly towards me, "Rena, please?"

Something broke inside and I couldn't blame it on the wind. My eyes watered from hearing his voice. I knew this was a huge effort for him to try to get my attention this morning. Besides, it was time to stop running. Eventually, Trey and I had to have the conversation I'd been avoiding. I needed him to understand.

Just not right now.

I cleared my throat which felt thick. "I'm on my way to the office. I have some important details to share with Clay this morning. Can we catch up later?"

Trey's smile didn't waver. He stepped closer to me, his eyes locked on mine. "I'm sure you haven't had breakfast yet. I know a cup of coffee would be helpful."

I bit my lip, I hadn't thought to set the coffeemaker last night. There was no need to try to figure out how Trey knew I was on the run without coffee. We'd always had this connection since we were younger. Despite the years that passed without being around each other, we'd reconnected as if time hadn't moved on.

I returned the smile, "You know me too well. I was going to grab Starbucks on the way."

He looked at his watch, "How about a steaming cup from Huddle House? You can catch some real breakfast."

"Trey..."

"Look, I know the office doesn't officially open until nine-thirty. It's almost eight o'clock. Surely you can spare me a few minutes before you jump into being super detective today. Please, Rena."

How can I refuse a man who knew how to say please? Not once, but twice.

I huffed. "Sure. I'll follow you over."

He blinked.

I held up my hands. "I promise. I will meet you there."

Trey raised his eyebrow and then turned to head back down the steps.

I was a tad bit hurt that he didn't believe me. It wasn't like I'd ever stood him up. I just made it my business not to be alone with him.

I purposely drove slower than necessary to the Huddle House. I spent my childhood and teenage years in love with Trey. After high school, we both went our separate ways, and life hadn't been good to me in the male area. I couldn't name one man that I'd had a good relationship with since Trey. Most of those relationships had left me scarred and unwilling to chance my feelings with another man.

Not even Trey.

Since I returned home a year ago, we'd been on a tightrope as we reestablished our friendship. Something lingered between the two of us now that we were older, but so much had happened during the twenty-five years we'd spent apart. It seemed ludicrous to even try to be more than friends.

Our senior year in high school, I dated a guy I knew Trey hated. My goal was to finally capture my best friend's attention. Well, I did, but the plan failed miserably and our friendship took a huge hit. When we graduated, Trey left for college and I began my long industrious career of one bad relationship after another.

The boyfriend that came between me and Trey was later shot and killed. He'd always been bad news, but no one deserved to die like that.

One year later, on the rebound and still grief stricken from the tragedy, I married a hometown guy. After an argument left me bruised and battered, I divorced him after a year. All of this happened before I'd even turned twenty-one. I managed to finish up my degree at UNC and became a junior reporter at WYNN.

Interestingly enough, my second time at the altar was with Trey's half-brother. That marriage didn't last long either.

Seemed like most of my life I'd chased after Trey in my own way, seeking his qualities in other men.

Now the tables had turned. He was chasing me, and I was running.

I know... complicated. That was me.

My stomach quivered as I climbed out of my car. I knew hunger pains weren't the cause. That late night lasagna still seemed to be sitting in my stomach, along with other things that were weighing heavily on me this morning.

I can't believe Trey is doing this now.

I entered Huddle House and found Trey waving at me from the back. I nodded at the usual customers as I made my way over to the booth and sat down without looking at him, even though I knew his eyes were still on me.

I'd let my natural hair grow out, and today I opted to tie a bright purple scarf around my twist-out. I had added some lip gloss to my lips before leaving the house. I was a far cry from the woman I used to be who spent many days in front of a camera, never daring to not have my hair extensions and make-up perfectly intact.

"Thanks for meeting with me," he started the conversation. "Feels like we keep missing each other."

I peered at Trey, tucking my hands under me so I wouldn't fidget. I was forty-three years old, but somehow being around this man always made me revert back to the twelve year old who used to sneak stares at him. I turned my attention to the glossy white menu in front of me. "I've been busy with cases. There is no shortage of cheaters in Georgetown and the surrounding areas."

He laughed. "I bet. I'm glad the private detective business is working out for you." Trey leaned over and his spicy cologne wafted towards my nose. "I was starting to think you were avoiding me."

I stared at Trey unable to respond. His dimple stood out against his freshly shaved face. I'd teased him mercilessly about getting rid of the beard which had been tinged with gray. He'd finally listened to me. Without the beard, he looked younger.

A flash of the young man who was my best friend many, many years ago almost had me wanting to cry again. I'd made up my mind that we would never be more than friends. The more he pushed the issue, the more I would dig in my heels. It wasn't something I enjoyed doing. In fact, it was slowly killing me not to just give in. Being alone with this man was not good for either one of us.

Trey had always been a good man, but now he was so much more. He was a godly man. A minister. He had a high standing in the community.

Me? I was over forty, no kids, twice-divorced and my past stayed beside me like a BFF. I'd used my body in ways I was not proud of. I'd done things I could never let Trey find out about.

After my fall three years ago, I'd asked the Lord into my heart. Laying in the hospital bed for far too long, feeling shattered, I truly knew Jesus as my Savior. There was no other way I would have made it past my injuries or the loss of my career as a reporter. I wouldn't have had the courage to move back home after all these years and face my past.

No matter how hard I tried, I couldn't picture me ever being the kind of woman that should be by Trey's side.

I tilted my head. "Like I said, I've been busy. Between choir and the youth ministry, you're not exactly without anything to do either, Minister Evans."

I couldn't help but remind him. Him chasing me wasn't a good idea.

He nodded. "You're right. This time of the year, with the holidays approaching, it's only going to get worse. I just miss spending time with you. Seems a few months ago, we just stopped all of sudden."

That's because a few months ago, we kissed. The kind of kiss that begged for so much more.

My cheeks grew warm at the mere memory. The past me would have had no problem moving past that kiss right to the bedroom. How many nights had I laid awake or woken up with thoughts of a not-so-clothed Trey?

Minister Trey Evans.

The waitress showed up at our table saving me from my wretched thoughts. I dipped my head towards the menu.

A familiar voice over my head stated, "I haven't seen you two together in a while."

I lifted my head and croaked, "Iris… good morning to you too. How are you?"

Iris Jenkins was the mother of Trey's son, Joseph. She kept the boy from Trey for years before he found out about his son last year. They were cordial to each other, but Trey struggled with bitterness towards Iris. She'd stolen so many years from him with his son.

I noticed Trey's eyes were glued to the menu, not looking at me or her.

Turning my attention back to Iris, I asked, "How's Joseph doing?"

Her smile was strained. In order to not get into a custody battle with Trey, they both took turns with Joseph. He had a room at each of their houses. "He's still doing good with the latest medicine.

"That's great." Joseph had sickle cell disease and his bouts were painful to watch. I added, "I'm glad the medicine is working for him."

Iris asked, "Trey, did you want the usual?"

Trey murmured, "Yeah."

I knew his usual plate consisted of grits, scrambled eggs and two pieces of bacon. Apparently, Iris knew that too. Despite the fact they shared a child, that's where the conversation between them ended.

I caught Iris' eyes, which were blank. "I will just stick with coffee."

She nodded and walked over to another table.

Now more than ever, I wished Trey had never showed up at my door this morning. I managed to get into his drama with Iris last year. I remembered his fury at Iris. Now, he treated the mother of his child with a cool politeness. He was determined to co-parent the son he was still getting to know. Part of my reasons for keeping our relationship at bay was because I really liked their son, Joseph. The boy loved having his dad in his life, and I'm sure the strain between his parents didn't help.

Iris made sure we had all we needed, and I observed Trey as he eyed Iris walking away. I wasn't sure how to read the expression on his face. It was a mixture of anger and relief. Maybe he felt the awkwardness that I felt since he'd showed up at my door.

He turned his attention to me, "Shall we pray?"

I nodded and bowed my head.

"Father God, thank you for the meal we're about to eat. Bless the hands that prepared it. Blessed the food that it nourishes our body and carries us through this morning. Lord, thank you for our friendship. We ask this in Jesus name. Amen."

Amen. I sipped my coffee in silence as I watched Trey eat. He didn't seem to mind that we weren't talking as he scooped up eggs and grits from his plate. His prayer lingered with me. *So, he thought of us as friends too?*

I couldn't stand it any longer. "You know we've been apart from each other for over twenty-five years.

We can survive not seeing each other for periods of time."

He paused from chewing. "Of course. Even though we lost touch for a few years, our friendship is just as strong."

I licked my lips, dreading what was about to slip from them. "You understand that I can't offer you anything more." I leaned in and stared at him. "I'm good with my life for the first time in a long time. I don't want any complications."

He looked out the window before turning to face me. I caught a brief flash of hurt in his eyes. "Are you saying I complicate your life, Rena?"

I grabbed the carafe at the end of the table and poured more coffee. "That's not what I'm saying. I just want us to enjoy being reunited as friends is all I'm saying."

We remained quiet after my statement. The awkwardness was driving me to bolt straight to my car. Last night was still on my mind, and though I know Trey needed my attention, I had some pressing matters.

Trey sat back in the booth not looking at me. "I will get the bill. I know you need to run. Thanks for joining me."

Feeling like he'd dismissed me, I cringed before I reached over and grabbed his hand.

He looked at my hand on his and then at me.

The hurt on his face made my eyes water.

Come on, Trey!

I wrapped both my hands around his hand. "Look, let's catch up later, okay. I'm sorry for being like this right now, but I have some really important stuff to share with Clay. I'm just anxious because this case is different from what I've been working on."

My eyes pleaded with him until I saw his dimple appear again.

"Okay, maybe we can grab dinner together?"

"You got it. Let me know when and I'll be there." As I rushed out of the restaurant, I felt my breath coming faster. The cold air felt good against my burning eyes.

I truly loved that man. Lord, knows I was trying to save him from me, but I wasn't doing a very good job. It was hard to push away someone I wanted so badly most of my life.

Chapter Four

Thursday, 9:16 am

Clayton Matthews stood over my desk as I showed him the photos I'd taken the night before. My brother-in-law wasn't one to show emotion on his face. Probably one of the reasons he was a sought-after divorce attorney, but as I peered up at his face, I was quite satisfied to see the same look of disgust that I felt all night. With two young daughters of his own, Clay seemed more heated than usual.

He turned his face away. "You did a good job with these, Rena. Can you print some copies so we can share with Mrs. Peters?"

"Sure. When is Judith coming in?"

Clay wiped his brow as he peered down at his watch. "In about an hour. She's been really antsy about getting these photos." He stepped back and folded his arms. "I have to tell you, I'm a bit apprehensive and that's saying a lot for me."

I gulped. "She knew her husband had been cheating on her, but you think seeing her daughter's friend is really going to be hard on her?"

Clay nodded. "You know I actually met Samantha one day when I took Judith some papers. Both girls came in to say hello. I remember Judith remarking that Samantha was like a daughter to her." His eyebrow furrowed. "The divorce is hard enough, but man, this is going to tear the entire family to pieces."

I agreed. "I still would like to know why Edwin would pursue his daughter's friend. I mean she's an attractive young woman, but his moral compass must be pretty low. It makes me wonder what else he's been doing."

Clay glanced at me as he began to walk out of my small office. "I've heard rumblings about Edwin's finances, but I didn't want to dig too deep."

I leaped up from my chair. "Why not? Don't you need an accurate look at his finances to determine Judith's settlement?" I followed Clay into the large receptionist area where his long-time secretary, Agnes Baker was lining up coffee cups.

Clay walked over. "Good morning, Agnes. Did you sleep well last night?"

Agnes peered at me, her eyes sharp. I never understood why Agnes was warm and friendly to everyone else but me. It wasn't like I took over any of her duties. She managed the office, and I found the evidence Clay needed.

"I did sleep better last night," she responded to her boss. "The cold weather actually helps. All that humidity wasn't good for my asthma."

Clay smiled, "It does feel like we will get some cooler weather at least for a while."

I wanted us to continue our conversation, but I knew Clay was careful not to mention too much in front of Agnes. She was a competent employee, but she did like to share a bit too much information which made her a typical gossip. And Judith Peters was a private woman despite her husband's prominent place in the community. Judith was the current principal at McDonald Elementary School, the same school my Aunt C served as a fourth grade teacher and later the principal. Aunt C retired a decade ago, so Judith had been in that position for some time now. I remember the image my Aunt C worked hard to keep. With Judith's standing in the school district, she was probably wanted her divorce to be finalized quietly. She'd stayed with the man this long, I wondered what made her file for divorce now.

Unfortunately, Judith married a man who didn't share her vision of keeping their lives from the public eye. With what we had to share with Judith today, life was about to get even uglier for the school principal, as well as her two children. I was feeling bad about capturing the photos, but my melancholic feelings were mainly towards Samantha Livingston who I felt was more like a victim. I replayed the events from last night in my head again, Samantha had slapped Edwin first. Was she ashamed of being there? Did the man say something to make her feel even worse?

I couldn't get the fear in her eyes out of my head. Nor the bruising around her neck. Edwin could have easily killed the young woman. Did guilty thoughts of his daughter finally creep into his mind at the last minute? Or was the distraction I provided last night the only thing that stopped him?

For the first time, since taking on cases where I had to find evidence against a spouse, I actually felt like my presence had a purpose.

Samantha walked away. Scared and bruised, but she walked away from a monster.

Now, we need to take that monster down.

I grabbed another cup of coffee. I had to give it Agnes, she made the best coffee. While I'd already had a cup at the Huddle House with Trey, I needed her strong brew to get me through the rest of the morning.

My mind briefly flashed to Trey's hurt expression from this morning. I shook my head. I would deal with Trey later. I had to focus on this case. I trailed Clay back to his office and closed the door behind me.

"Are you just going to leave me hanging? Is part of this huge tension between Edwin and Judith over finances?"

Clay sat behind his desk and sighed. "Partly. I haven't been able to get Edwin to fully disclose all of his income. I suspect ..." He held up his finger as if he were scolding me, "and this is just a theory."

I slipped into a chair in front of his desk.

He leaned in. "I don't think the businessman makes all of his money legally within Waterway Commercial Real Estate. Clearly, real estate is his business, and he makes out well with these coastal properties—"

"But he's getting some other kind of income. I knew it." I slapped my hand on my thigh. "There has to be more to a man who sinks as low as the one I saw last night. What do you think he's dealing in?"

Clay shook his head. "I don't want to get too deep into this. I don't have proof, and it's been hard enough to get the man to be open. Besides, what's most important to Judith is her kids. Their son, Ethan just turned thirteen. He still lives at home, and Judith's main concern is being granted full custody."

I sat back. "That makes sense. She will need child support too. You still need a better view of his finances."

Clay sighed, "Child support isn't really an issue. Judith comes from money herself. In fact, I'm pretty sure Judith helped Edwin establish his business early on in his career. She's not involved at all in Waterway, but I believe she has a stake in it. That's where Edwin is going to fight her."

I knew this divorce case was going to be a war. It also explained how the Peters could afford two homes in the million dollar range.

Clay peered down, flipping through a stapled document on his desk, "I'm looking at what his lawyer is offering. It's not bad, but I do sense there's hidden funds. Even Judith mentioned she knows he's raking in extra cash from somewhere, but she's not clear where else to look. It's not about the money to her, she wants to make sure her children's futures are solid."

I balked. "Come on, Clay, this is right up my alley. I'm your investigator. Let me dig into his finances."

He shook his head. "No, Bev would have my head if she knew this work was going to lead you into danger."

I sat up straighter. *Danger.*

"What? I didn't get my private investigator's license just to be taking photos of cheating spouses, Clay." I stood. "Seeing Edwin assault Samantha last night didn't sit right with me, and then to later find out she's like a close family member… I've seen egocentric men like Edwin before. The man is drunk on power, worshipping the money god. And it's obvious he's like some pervert."

Clay held up his hands. "Whoa. Cool it, Rena. We have to remember that Samantha went there on her own, and she's at least the same age as Janine, who I know is twenty."

I eyed my brother-in-law. "She's a twenty year old that has been coerced in some way by a powerful man old enough to be her father. You don't think she's a victim? You saw the photos."

Clay sighed, "I'm as disgusted as you are. But I'm a divorce attorney, my client's needs and wishes come first. I'm only here to get what my client is owed from her cheating husband. We will show Judith all the photos. Good thinking calling the police last night. I'm sure there will be a report about the incidence. Samantha can come forward to charge Edwin."

If she isn't too scared.

I failed to mention my trip to Samantha's apartment to Clay. I freelanced for him as an investigator. Clay didn't dictate any other cases I decided to pick up. Of course, until now, I didn't have any other cases. But that was about to change.

I had a feeling Samantha would never come forward about last night. Now knowing her closeness to the Peters family, Samantha had just as much to hide.

What would the young woman do when her best friend found out about the affair?

A knock on Clay's door broke my thoughts. I turned to see Agnes at the door, her face distressed. "Clay, Mrs. Peters arrived early. Do you want me to send her in now or do you need more time?"

Clay stood. "You can send her in now." He looked at me, "Can you get those photos ready?"

"Coming right up." As I left Clay's office, I glanced over at Judith Peters. The woman sat with her back rim-rod straight in the waiting room chair as if bracing herself for what she was about to learn. I normally didn't stick around when Clay talked to clients.

My curiosity about this case made me want to stick around for the fireworks today.

BITTERSWEET MOTIVES

Chapter Five

Thursday, 10:32 am

Judith Peters looked through the photos that were hot off my printer. For a full minute, she didn't utter a word. The range of emotions on her face left me wanting to grab a box of tissues. She looked up at Clay. Her mouth was open as if she wanted to ask a question, but she quickly shut her mouth as her lips formed a tight line. The tears shimmering in her eyes descended down her face creating streaks in her makeup.

Judith wasn't what I called a beautiful woman, but she was a woman who knew how to artfully apply makeup and kept her short hair layered to perfection so that it laid in all the right places around her face. In her early fifties, Judith's hair was light brown with not a hint of gray. She looked like an astute administrator of an elementary school.

She wore a tailored camel colored pantsuit with a cream colored blouse underneath. I glanced down at her brown leather boots. Everything about her was perfect except the emotions warring on her face.

Judith stuffed the photos back in the envelope and tossed it on Clay's desk. "When were these taken?"

Clay sat with his hands clasped together on his desk. He cleared his throat and nodded in my direction, "Ms. Manchester captured these last night at the family house on Pawleys Island where Edwin is staying."

Judith focused her eyes on me and clasped her hands together, acknowledging my presence for the first time. "Tell me what you saw. I want the full report."

I responded, "Okay. I followed Mr. Peters from his office building. At first, I thought he was going to the bar he frequents, but he ventured down Highway 17. I tailed him to Pawleys Island, then to the house. About twenty minutes after Mr. Peters arrived, the young woman showed up. I snapped the photos from behind the house. You can see the open windows allowed me to capture the shots."

Judith nodded as if she was absorbing my words. "Was this the first time?"

"First time seeing Peters with the young lady? Yes." Curious about what Mrs. Peters was thinking, I decided to prompt her. "Do you know her?"

Of course, I knew the woman was Samantha Livingston, but I wanted to know if Judith would reveal her identity.

She rubbed her hands across her pants as if she was pressing out some imaginary wrinkles. When she responded, her voice was hoarse as if her throat hurt. "She's like a daughter. She just turned twenty last month...my daughter's best friend since third grade." Judith's voice cracked.

I noticed her fists were balled up in her lap.

The nervous energy in the room was palpable. Like something, or in this case, someone was about to explode. I looked over at Clay, glad I wasn't the only one feeling anxious. He leaned forward, "Judith, are you okay? Can we get you something? I know this has been a shock."

Fists still balled, Judith shook her head. She croaked, "I expected him to be with someone. Some floozy. He always had somebody around who would call him all times of the night. They were bold, calling the house phone. But this…" her voice dropped to a whisper.

I stepped closer to make sure I could hear.

She looked down and unclenched her fists, remaining quiet for a few seconds. Then, she lifted her head and looked back and forth between us. "I don't know what to do with this. I wish you'd caught him with someone else. Anyone else?"

Judith stood and paced the room. "I treated her like my daughter. I knew she had some tendencies like her mother, but she—"

"Her mother?" I interrupted, not liking where this was going. I was that young woman in this town many years ago, once thought of being just like my dad. My dad was a ladies' man and not the world's best father. His reputation haunted me even when I arrived back in town last year. I wasn't too happy when people threw someone under the bus because of who their parents were.

Judith whipped around, her face flushed. "She was a floozy. A drug addict. She overdosed when Sam was ten. The poor child was taken to foster care for a while before her grandmother could get custody. She lived with us on and off whenever her grandmother was too frail to care for her. We took her in permanently after her grandmother died."

I knew I probably shouldn't, but I couldn't help myself. "I don't want you take this the wrong way, Mrs. Peters, but your husband is the person with the power here. The father figure."

Judith turned towards me, eyes blazing.

Clay cleared his throat, but I kept going. "Samantha is a victim here. I don't know how long this has been going on, but your husband should have never approached her this way. Perhaps she felt like she didn't have a choice."

Judith stared at me, but I stood my ground. I'd kept a few photos out of the envelope. I glanced at Clay who was slowly shaking his head at me. "You should see these photos too."

I showed her the photo of Edwin with his hands around Samantha's throat.

Judith sucked in a breath like she'd been punched in the stomach. She sank down in the chair, her hands trembling.

I powered on as if I needed to somehow defend Samantha. "I called the police. I didn't know if he was going to kill her. She may have come to the house willingly for whatever absurd reason, but that was too far. She's a victim. Even if her mother had some kind of reputation, your husband wasn't being very fatherly to a young woman who grew up alongside his daughter."

Judith cried out, placing her face in her hands.

Clay stood, "Serena, that's enough. I think it's best you leave now."

"I'm sorry, Clay. She needed to know. That girl was wrong for meeting with Edwin, but she got traumatized in the process. Who knows how many other women have been abused like this?"

Judith cried harder. Clay came around the desk and patted her on the back. His eyes urged me to leave. Noting the flashes of anger in my brother-in-law's face and Judith increasing cries of devastation, I walked out and closed the door behind me.

Agnes was standing behind her desk looking concerned. "Is she alright? I know that husband of hers is a brute."

I stepped away from the mahogany door, trying to shut out the muffled cries. "She's taking my findings pretty hard."

Agnes shook her head. "I hate to say this, but she shouldn't be surprised. Edwin Peters always had a flavor of the month. Everyone knew it too. I'm sure she did too, although she acted like her life was perfect."

Passing Agnes, I muttered. "People can always surprise us." I closed the door to my small office and sat. Guilt etched into my mind. I hated to upset Judith, but neither she nor Clay saw what I saw last night.

Samantha was more than just the *other woman*.

I believe she showed up at Edwin's house for another reason. When the young woman slapped Edwin, I interpreted that as her fighting back in her own way. Instead, she escaped, scared out of her mind with the remnants of a man's hands around her throat. She was a victim.

Victimized by a man she probably trusted at one time.

Chapter Six

Thursday, 7:20 pm

I'd barely taken my shoes off before my doorbell rang. My thoughts went immediately to my morning conversation with Trey. I'd promised him dinner, but it was too soon. After today, I really didn't want to deal with anyone. I needed time to think. I had it in mind to reach out to the Samantha after I got home and rested. It had also been on my mind to run a background check on her too. I wanted to know more about her life and her own family. The young woman had been visibly scared, and I couldn't help but think the man that was supposed to be a father figure in her life had taken advantage of her. I also wondered how long it had been going on.

It deeply disturbed me that Samantha grew up in a household under a man who would pursue her sexually. That meant he'd done it before and I had a feeling it wasn't willingly.

The doorbell chimed again, and this time, whoever the insistent person was, held it down. "Alright, I'm coming." I yelled. My immediate sense was it could not be Trey at my door but a really obnoxious and annoying person.

Trey exhibited none of those traits.

I headed towards the front door, almost colliding with the cat as she took off down the hallway towards the bedroom. I shook my head; I had to admit having to jump over the feline whenever she needed to streak from a room kept me agile.

Wishing I could run and hide, like my cat, from whoever was terrorizing me with the doorbell, I peeked through the door and sucked in a breath.

This can't be good.

It'd been awhile since these two showed up at my house. Last year, when I witnessed a murder at a local convenience store, I saw more of these two than I cared. I unlatched the lock and opened the door, forcing a smile on my tired face. "This is a surprise."

Detective Oliver Baldwin and Detective Malcolm Moses stood on my porch, their faces grim. Moses was the shorter, stockier of the two; his dark brown bald head shone under my porch light. Baldwin, the older of the two men, was tall and appeared more gaunt than the last time I saw him. His graying temples were cut close, and while the man had to be approaching fifty, he still had a thick mane of hair.

Baldwin smiled, "May we come in, Serena?"

Baldwin was always the obvious good cop. I eyed Moses, who seemed to be seething with animosity. I got the impression Moses stayed angry when he was on the job. I had the good fortune to be around the man outside of work, and he was almost a different person. I opened the door wider. "I'm not sure what you need from me, but come in."

After both men ambled into my house, I closed the door and led them to the living room. Besides putting up a few of my paintings on the wall, I hadn't changed much since they visited me last year. Most of Aunt C's knickknacks and family photos still cluttered various areas of the living room. They'd grown on me and made the place more cozy, like home.

Moses jumpstarted the conversation before I could sit down. "Where were you last night, Rena?"

I frowned, deciding I might better stand for this conversation. I placed my hands on my hips, bracing myself. "Why are you questioning me about my whereabouts?"

Moses narrowed his eyes, "Don't make this difficult. Just let us know."

I crossed my arms. "I was out on a case. Tailing Ed... a person of interest for a client." This was a first for me, but I didn't think Clay would appreciate me spilling any confidential information about his client.

Moses and Baldwin shared a glance.

Baldwin asked, "So you were staking out a place? Where?"

I frowned before answering. I had a sneaky suspicion that I wasn't going to like the way this conversation was heading. "I was quite a few places. Around here in Georgetown, drove out to Pawleys Island and then drove back to town."

Moses glanced at Baldwin. "Pawleys Island?" He took out a notebook from inside his jacket and flipped it open. "Care to tell us who you were staking out?"

I watched him. "Let's just say the person I was tailing is a prominent businessman." Baldwin and Moses were detectives. Knowing them, they would probably figure it out. I still wasn't comfortable dropping names without talking to Clay.

Baldwin had also whipped a notepad out of his jacket pocket. "Was the address you were staking out 951 Foxborough Drive?"

I flinched before I could stop myself. "Where did you get that address?"

Baldwin smiled slightly, before his face turned serious again. "We're following up on this address."

Moses added, "We found out a domestic disturbance call was made to 9-1-1 around 7:54 pm from this same address. Do you know anything about that call?"

My stomach began to feel uneasy. "Yes, things got a little tense …"

Moses stared at me. "Were you a part of the domestic disturbance, Rena?"

I scoffed, "I was not."

"We do have the 9-1-1 recording from dispatch." He narrowed his eyes. "It sounds like you. I recognized your cell number too." He peered at his partner, "We also have a pretty good idea of who you were staking out last night. Just not why… We're hoping you can tell us more, especially about this young woman."

Alarms shot through my stomach. My head swung back and forth, staring at both detectives. Both of them were homicide detectives. Fear crept down my spine. I knew why they were here without them even having to tell me, and this knowledge made me weak in my knees.

Moses stepped forward and grabbed my arm as his eyes shifted to concern. "Rena, are you okay?"

Barely recognizing my voice, I squeaked out. "Did something happen to Samantha? Is this why you're here?"

I watched Moses and Baldwin share another glance, confirming my worst fear.

"Tell me." My voice went up, shocking me and the detectives. In a softer tone, I begged, "You two work homicide. Just tell me what happened to her."

"Rena," Moses held out his hands. "Samantha Livingston was found dead in her apartment this afternoon."

I gripped my hands together. "No, no… Who found her?" I slapped my hands on my head. "Was it him? Did he go back to finish her off?"

Baldwin frowned. "Him? Are you talking about the individual who owns the home you visited last night?"

Did Edwin actually kill her? The man lost his temper last night, but surely he wouldn't have drawn attention to himself like this after having the cop at his home. I thought about what was in my workbag, but I couldn't show them that. I was obligated by my investigations for Clay to keep my findings confidential. Clay wouldn't be happy if he knew I had printed off two copies of the photos. Especially, since I had the photos of Edwin wrapping his hands around Samantha's neck.

Now, the young woman was dead.

Wait, I didn't have to show them photos. They already knew about the 9-1-1 call, and there was a police report. This would get back to Edwin anyway.

Thank you, Lord!

I calmed my breath. "I called 9-1-1 last night because I saw my subject trying to harm Samantha." I purposely didn't say his name. "There should have been bruises around her throat. He was choking her."

Moses leaned over and whistled. "So just to confirm, you were on a stakeout around Edwin Peter's home and you saw him assault Samantha?"

I grimaced. "Yes. I didn't reveal myself to the police, but I was hoping Samantha would press charges and an official police report would be filed." Then it dawned on me. "How did you know Samantha was at Pawleys Island or about the 9-1-1 call?"

Moses answered, "We were able to look at Samantha's GPS in her car. She had keyed in this address at Pawleys Island. We talked to a neighbor who confirmed seeing Samantha's car, a lime green Beetle, in the front of the house. They also claimed a police cruiser showed up last night too."

I wondered which neighbor. Did they see me snooping around the house too?

Baldwin interrupted my thoughts, "What happened after the patrol car showed up?"

Numbness started to creep up my body. "Samantha left. She was shook, but she walked out on her own and headed home."

Moses glowered at me. "How do you know she headed home?"

I wasn't happy with where this conversation was going. My shoulders sank, the tension of the news still piercing my brain. "I followed her to her apartment. I wanted to make sure she was alright."

Baldwin prodded, "Did you talk to her?"

I nodded. "I could see the bruises around her neck." I touched my own neck. "She was so scared."

Moses inquired, "Did you go inside her apartment?"

"No, I didn't get past the front door. She stepped out, closed the door slightly behind her and we talked outside." I let out a breath. "Wait, are you trying to pin this on me? Am I a suspect?"

Baldwin shook his head, "We just want to know where you were."

Adrenaline surged through me as I paced my small living room floor. But I didn't have far to pace with Moses and Baldwin standing nearby. It felt more like I was circling the same patch of carpet than pacing. "Look, I was on a job. I'd never seen Samantha until last night. I saw her getting assaulted with my own eyes, and I called 9-1-1. Like any decent human being, I wanted to check on her. She was scared. Me showing up probably scared her more. I didn't go inside her apartment, and I barely got a glimpse inside before she shut the door behind her." I stood still and caught my breath. I spun to face both detectives. "How did she die?"

Baldwin ignored my question, "So when you were outside her door, that's when you gave her your card?"

I narrowed my eyes. "Yeah. How do you know I gave her my card?"

Baldwin pulled out an evidence bag from his coat pocket. "This was found inside the victim's dress pocket. We wanted to know why she had your card and when she obtained it."

I peered down, looking at my business card inside the plastic evidence bag.

My throat closed up as my eyes watered at the sight. I stuttered, "I guess she stuffed it in her pocket after I left." Moisture ran down my cheeks. "I was thinking I would reach out to her tonight to see how she was doing. She should have charged him with assault." I wiped my face with the back of my hand. "Are you going to tell me how she died?"

Baldwin answered, "We don't have all the preliminaries from the coroner yet, but she appeared to have fallen backwards. It's possible she was pushed. Her neck was broken. If it wasn't for her friend stopping by to check on her this afternoon, she may have not been found for days."

I wiped at my face. "Pushed? So someone came after I left or would this assailant have already been there?"

Moses' bad cop stance was gone. He seemed more weary than anything. "Don't know," he shrugged. "There was definitely some kind of altercation in the apartment which makes us think Samantha wasn't alone when she had her fatal fall. We're trying to piece together the timeline. Unfortunately, none of her neighbors have been very helpful. No one heard or saw any noise or activity in her apartment."

Last night was Wednesday. I thought about my sister who was very active in her church. Wednesday night was usually bible study night. As I thought back to last night, I remembered how quiet it had been. Not a sound of life coming from any of the apartments. Having lived in several apartments in my life, the building materials that went into those walls were hardly soundproof.

My knees trembled. I made way over to the chair that my Aunt C considered her favorite and had since become my favorite and sank down. Thoughts whirred in my mind. Edwin Peters had his hands around Samantha's throat. Then I thought about Judith Peters. Earlier today, I watched as the woman had a near breakdown in Clay's office. The photos of Samantha with her husband had her shook.

She had some tendencies like her mother...

Judith's immediate comparison of Samantha to her mother's past history still didn't sit well with me. What did the woman do after she left our office this morning?

Now, I wasn't sure who killed Samantha. I looked at Moses and Baldwin. "Do you have an approximate time of death?"

Baldwin shook his head. "The coroner will let us know his findings in the morning. Preliminary examination put her death last night between nine o'clock and midnight."

The room seemed to swim, and I gripped the arms of the chair. "I'd just left there. I helped her escape with her life from one place for her to die in her own apartment."

I looked up at Baldwin and Moses. With what they knew, they had to question Edwin. Would Edwin have left the island to finish off Samantha? That didn't seem likely.

What about Judith? She seemed surprised by the photos, but did she really not know that her husband had been pursuing her daughter's best friend? Suppose she'd confronted Samantha last night and pretended her outrage to Clay and me earlier today.

I didn't know if my thoughts made much sense, but I had to get to Clay. He needed to know that his divorce case had just taken a turn for the worse.

Chapter Seven

Thursday, 9:04 pm

I banged on the door, my body still shaking with a mixture of anger and shock. My sister appeared at the door ready for bed. She wore a housecoat over pink polka-dot pajamas and a bright fuchsia scarf was tied neatly around her head.

Bev opened the screen door, her eyes wide with fear. "Rena, what's wrong? Why are you here so late?"

It wasn't that late, in my opinion, but I knew my punctual younger sister loved her routines. Even when we were children, Bev never strayed from her schedule. Where I would stay up until the early morning, she was in bed not too long after nine o'clock. And her girls, Brittany and Tiffany went to bed at eight-thirty.

I entered through the open door. The warmth of her house enveloped me, but I still felt chilled from the news I'd just received. I waited for Bev to lock the door back and reset the alarm. When she turned to me, I reached out to her. "I'm sorry, I should have called. But I didn't know what to do, so I thought it better to just come here. Is Clay still up?"

"Yes, I am."

I whirled to see my brother-in-law with a mug in his hand. He too had a robe wrapped around a pair of pajamas. I looked back and forth from my sister and her husband thinking once again how alike these two were. I was glad one of us in the family had a happily ever after marriage.

I let out a breath. "I'm sorry. I needed to know if you knew what happened, Clay?"

He frowned. "No, what's going on?"

I glanced at Bev's concerned face. I didn't know how much my brother-in-law shared with my sister. "It's about today's client meeting."

Bev asked, "Do you want something hot to drink, Rena? It's cold out there and you're only dressed in jeans and a hoodie."

I hadn't given much thought to putting on warm clothes. After the detectives left my home, it was all I could do not to run over to the crime scene. In the end, I didn't think I could handle it, not that anyone would let me anywhere near the place.

"Sure," I answered, "coffee would be great. I'm going to be up for a while anyway."

As soon as my sister was out of earshot, I sprang towards Clay. "Samantha Livingston is dead."

Eyes startled behind his glasses, Clay stepped back. "What? How do you know this? I watched the news tonight."

"I'm sure she'll make the eleven o'clock news."

Clay nodded. "Come in the living room, there's no need to stand in the hallway. Tell me what you know."

I followed Clay into the plush living room. My sister was a bit old school. She preferred the girls to hang out in the family room which was down the hall near their bedrooms. The living room was definitely more showcase than lived in. I sat daintily on the cream colored sofa and explained what I had learned.

"She was found this afternoon by a friend. The detectives on the case are Baldwin and Moses. They came by to see me."

Clay frowned. "Why would they come to see you? Did they trace the 9-1-1 call to your cell phone? They wouldn't have had time to do that."

I sighed. "They found my business card on Samantha. She had it in her pocket."

Clay's eyes flashed, "What?"

Bev came into the living room. "The coffee is ready." She glanced at both of us. "You sure you don't want to come in the kitchen? It's a lot warmer in there."

I smiled, catching my sister's subtle way of saying there was no way I was drinking coffee in her living room. "Sure."

I followed my sister to the kitchen and remained quiet as she fixed my coffee the way I liked, two sugars and cream. She sat the steaming mug in front of me. "I'm going to check on the girls. I put them to bed an hour ago, but I still hear giggling. If they find out you're here, I'm not sure I will be able to keep them in the bed."

I chuckled. While I didn't have kids, Brittany and Tiffany often spent weekends with me and more than made up for my childless life. Whenever my nieces were around, I was reminded of how often I ran off to be at Aunt C's house when I was their age. To avoid my stepfather's wrath, I practically lived in my aunt's home in high school.

"I won't be long," I assured my sister. "I just wanted to alert Clay to some changes in a case."

Bev nodded and then came over to peck me on top of the head. I was seven years older, but I often felt like my younger sister mothered me. "Be sure to get some sleep. I can tell when you're not sleeping. You know it starts to affect your head."

I sighed. "Yes, mother."

Bev rolled her eyes at me. "I'm just looking out for you. Lord knows, you won't do it."

She had a point. I was careless, but it was my life.

Once my sister left the kitchen, I glanced at Clay who had been staring at his phone. "What are you looking at?"

Clay responded, "I was texting a contact to see if I could get copies of the police reports." He looked at me, his expression sharp and focused. "You said you gave Samantha your business card. When?"

I licked my lips. "I probably should have told you that I followed her home last night. We had a brief talk and I gave her my card."

He shook his head. "Why? So that means she knew you were there taking photos?"

"I didn't spill what I was doing or who it was for. Besides, if you were in my shoes, you would have checked on her too. The man tried to strangle her... She was scared, Clay."

Before he could respond, I gripped the warm mug. "Judith is probably going to be questioned too. I didn't tell them, but they are going to figure out I was on assignment for her divorce case against Edwin."

Clay's forehead held deep frown marks. He held up his mug but didn't take a sip. "What else did you tell them?"

"I didn't mention anything about Judith. It's just that the timing... This afternoon, Judith was emotional in a scary way. Don't you agree? She looked like she wanted to explode." I leaned in and brought my voice down barely above a whisper. "They think Samantha had an altercation inside her apartment with someone. Looks like she was pushed. Her neck was broken."

Clay sipped his coffee, staring at me as my information sank in.

"You should know the detectives claimed the coroner's preliminary findings were that Samantha was killed last night. That would have been before Judith was presented with the photos. But I just wonder if Judith was completely oblivious all this time to Edwin pursuing Samantha? The woman had animosity against Samantha's mother. There had to be a reason for that."

I gulped down more coffee, finishing the cup. "I just thought you should be prepared or find a way to make sure Judith has representation for when she's questioned. This has become way more than a bitter divorce. Somebody murdered Edwin's ..."

I couldn't say it. I didn't feel right calling Samantha a mistress. It didn't seem like that tawdry label should be associated with the young woman at all. Her social media photos presented her as being a pretty sweet young woman with a love of all things fashion. The scared young woman last night didn't seem like she'd come to seduce Edwin. If anything, she was probably reaching out to him and things took a bad turn.

Clay invaded my thoughts, "Judith wouldn't go that far."

"How do you know that? She never thought the woman Edwin was seeing would have been their daughter's friend, either. A girl they both treated like their own daughter." I spun the mug in my hand. "I'm telling you, Judith needs a tight alibi and so does Edwin. Both of them had motive to confront her. In a fit of anger, the confrontation could have gone wrong. Judith could have been trying to protect her daughter."

I hoped Judith didn't go anywhere near that girl. The person who needed to go down was Edwin Peters. He was the center of the family's downward spiral.

What was the man thinking? Of all the women he had to mess with, why did he choose Samantha Livingston? What happened to make him want to harm her? Did he ultimately kill her?

Chapter Eight

Thursday, 11:32 pm

Back home in bed, I cranked up the electric blanket. Despite the cat bed in the corner, the calico ball snored near me on the other side of the queen-sized bed. I'd never owned a pet the entire time I lived on my own in Charlotte. And I admit, I missed the feline when she wasn't on the bed. The glow from my laptop was all that lit the room as I typed in anything I could find about Samantha Livingston.

I found myself surfing the same social media platforms I had visited the previous night, but tonight, my perusal felt eerie causing me to bury even deeper under the covers. There was something unsettling about reading the final social media post from a deceased person. I read Samantha's final post over and over again, unable to comprehend fully what the young woman left as her last words.

You think you know people, but you can never really know them, can you? People are always surprising us, and the results are always devastating. I'm so tired of being disappointed.

Samantha's last post was posted around six o'clock Wednesday evening. A little over an hour before she arrived at the Peters' beach house. Hundreds of people had liked the post, and the post had over one hundred comments, many agreeing with the young woman.

To me, this post was also a clear indication that perhaps Samantha had been dreading her meeting with Edwin Peters. He seemed to be a pretty big disappointment in her life. What a meetup that was for the young woman. Barely escaping with her life.

The man had the opportunity to drive back into Georgetown to visit her. I had a hard time fathoming that Samantha would open her door to Edwin Peters.

Who did she open the door for? It had to have been someone she knew and trusted.

Of course, she didn't know me, but knowing that I'd seen her predicament was what encouraged Samantha to open her door to me. I knew her secret. Or at least part of it. A lot of my assumptions of why Samantha showed up at the Peters' waterfront home were based on what I interpreted via my camera lens. With her dead now, my perceptions didn't feel fair or just.

As I scrolled through the comments, I started to notice around five o'clock on Thursday, the comments started to change. One comment from Amir Wright stood out to me.

Oh, Samantha. What happened? I can't believe you're gone now.

I wondered how this person knew Samantha was already gone. Moses and Baldwin mentioned a friend found her body Thursday afternoon in her apartment. After this initial comment from Amir Wright, the posts started to reflect sorrow over Samantha's passing. I left Samantha's final post and went back to her profile. The more I scrolled, the more I saw people posting their sorrows to Samantha's page. I doubted many of her followers knew the real Samantha. They probably mourned the persona she displayed on social media.

I got up and turned on the lamp on my nightstand. It was essential to find out who were Samantha's real friends. They might have clues about what happened to her. Maybe someone knew of her dealings with the much older Edwin Peters.

I grabbed my trusty notebook from the old wooden desk in the corner of the room. The desk belonged to Aunt C. I recalled many nights coming into her room and watching her grading papers or writing in her notebook at the desk. I ran my hand across the desk before settling in the chair which had a well-worn, but comfortable red cushion. I flipped open my notebook to a blank page and grabbed a black ink pen. The investigative reporter side of me wanted to skim down the listing of who, what and why.

I loved my laptop, but there was nothing compared to pen and paper to get my thoughts rattling. I had a trunkful of notebooks over the years from my reporting days and even a few journals. I didn't think I was that interesting, personally, but the people I had encountered over the years could help me write a very candid memoir.

It was after midnight according to the chimes from the nightstand clock. My eyes had grown sleepy despite my desire to write notes. My list so far wasn't very long. From comparing Samantha's Facebook and Instagram posts, she seemed to interact with a handful of people all the time. Despite her large amount of followers, Samantha's online popularity was obviously due to her love for fashion and makeup.

I placed an asterisk by the first person on my list. No surprise. Janine Peters was the number one person Samantha connected to online and offline. Tonight, Instagram and Facebook was quiet for Janine. She hadn't posted anything about her friend. In fact, her last post was from last Saturday night around 11:35 pm on Instagram. The two best friends were dressed pretty similar, wearing skintight jeans and shirts that showed off their toned mid-sections.

Janine's long straight black hair fell around her face, while Samantha's curly hair was pulled up on top of her head. Both girls resembled supermodels, tall and leggy. Janine was a bit more ample in the hips compared to Samantha's slim frame. I peered closer at the scene behind the girls. I could see people in the background, possibly on a dance floor. It appeared they were in some club.

Which brought me back to my encounter with Samantha last night. How long had Samantha been messing around with her best friend's dad? Was last night the first time or had she visited the businessman many times before? It was hard to imagine that a best friend could not be torn up inside, yet Samantha and Janine were smiling as if they didn't keep a secret in the world from each other.

The second person on my list was Amir Wright. I clicked over to his social media profile and was instantly smitten. Amir had the body of a lean athlete, with no trace of bulky muscles. He had to be a little over six feet, and his face was chiseled. But what stood out even more was his eyes. He appeared to have a mixture of Asian and African American heritage. No doubt, the man could turn heads. I found myself lingering a little too long on his shirtless photos.

Old habits don't die. Jesus, help me.

My desire to live the Christian life was clashing with my hormones, which apparently weren't dead yet. In a past life, I had no issues approaching a man like Amir.

Not only did his good looks fascinate me, but there were just as many photos of Samantha with Amir as there were with Janine. There were several photos of him in the middle of both women.

Was he a friend or a boyfriend? To which friend?

Surely if he was Samantha's boyfriend, she would have no reason to even consider looking at the much older Edwin Peters. Was the situation with Peters a money thing?

I stared at Amir. Something about him made him appear older than the two young women. I guessed he was in his mid-to-late twenties. A few minutes later, I jerked myself away from staring at the young man and closed the laptop with a snap.

My sudden movement disturbed my furball roommate. Callie stirred and glared at me, her feline eyes wide, then narrowing as if to scold me for disturbing her sleep.

"Sorry, you can go back to sleep now." I climbed back in the bed.

The old me had no problems leering at a good-looking man. Despite my past sexual trysts, I was a new woman now. I wouldn't let my mind go that way, not anymore, not ever again. My heart had been broken too many times, and I was guilty of leaving just as many broken hearts behind me.

Trey's face sprang to mind. After the way I'd left him Thursday morning at Huddle House, we needed to at least address the awkwardness that had settled on our relationship. Which was mainly my fault. If only he knew how damaged I really was, maybe he wouldn't chase me quite so hard.

I glanced over at the clock. It was approaching one in the morning, the time where my mind tended to wander to unhealthy thoughts.

I walked to the kitchen to grab a glass of water. After I gulped down the liquid, I regretted it. With age, I often woke up in the middle of the night to use the bathroom. I placed the glass in the sink, thinking I may as well stay up a while longer.

I grabbed my laptop again and climbed back under the covers which had grown cool. When I tapped the screen, Amir's bright smile stared back at me. I studied his face a bit more, hoping to keep my hormones in check this time. With the way he wore his goatee, the young man didn't seem a day over thirty, but he could definitely pass for twenty-five. Still, that put him a bit older than Samantha.

And way too young for me.

Ugh, I cringed and slapped the laptop closed again.

Where did that stupid thought come from?

I laid my head against the pillow, staring into the darkness that enveloped the bedroom. Images of the last time I saw Samantha assaulted my mind. The scared look in her eyes. The bruising around her neck. I needed to find out who caused Samantha's death. I'm not sure why I thought it had to be me. Moses and Baldwin were perfectly capable of solving this homicide case. It was their job.

But the girl died with my business card in her pocket.

I didn't know why that thought compelled me. Maybe the detectives finding my information and what I'd seen Wednesday night had forever connected me to Samantha.

I thought about the moments before Edwin grabbed Samantha by the throat. She'd reached out and slapped Edwin in the face first. The slap and whatever she said pushed Edwin over the edge.

What did he say to upset her?

I really wished I had the ability to put a listening device in the home. Clay wouldn't have approved; recordings weren't admissible in court. Still, having access to the conversation between the two would have been so helpful right now.

My mind continued to process information despite the fact that my body was drifting off to sleep. A group of faces rose in my mind from my earlier research before sleep finally overtook me. Janine, Amir and Samantha together, smiling at whoever was behind the camera.

Chapter Nine

Friday, November 9, 10:37 am

The next morning I drove to the place I knew I was not wanted. Thankfully, when I arrived at the Georgetown Police Department, neither Detective Baldwin nor Moses were around to kick me out. I approached the person I knew would spill what I needed to know. Back during my reporter days, I often intensely followed and reported crime stories. I believed in keeping a few friends in the police department. With the right person willing to spill, it made it easier to report the facts.

Deputy Larry Wilson happened to grow up with my dad, Dallas Robinson and was an old friend. My dad went the way of becoming a drunk and a ladies' man. He also died way too early, leaving me scarred from his already lack of presence in my life. For as long as I had known him, Deputy Wilson had always been a good guy. When my dad died, Larry was one of the people who looked after me and made sure I stayed on the straight and narrow. Even after my mom married my stepdad, Reverend Lawson, Larry still checked on me.

When I arrived back in town last year, after being away for almost twenty-five years, Larry was one of the first people to show up at Aunt C's house to make sure I was settled back home. I got the feeling Larry always had a thing for my aunt.

Close to retirement now, Larry was just waiting around for his pension. I wouldn't say he wasn't a good cop, though he'd definitely slacked off over the years. But that was his prerogative, he'd earned his time. Still, I could often count on him to pass along information to me that I wouldn't normally have had access to.

To make sure Larry was in a good mood, I bought an extra-large black coffee from Huddle House with me.

"Good morning, Larry." I pasted a grin on my face, gliding the coffee across the counter towards him.

Larry looked up from his desk. The scowl on his face disappeared when he saw me, and the crevices in his weathered brown face turned fatherly and warm. For a brief moment, I wondered what my dad would have looked like if he'd lived this long. This thought always invaded my mind when I met with Larry.

He stood from the chair, wincing as if his knees were bothering him. "Rena, what you doing here, girl? It's always good to see you."

I pushed the coffee closer to him. "I figured this would be better than what they're serving in that coffee maker behind you."

"Hey, I made that coffee myself." Larry picked up the cup and grinned at me before taking a sip. "Mmm, now that's some good coffee." He eyed me, "Let me guess, you must want something."

I pretended to be hurt by shifting my eyes down, but I slowly lifted my head to share a grin. "Just curious to know if anyone in the community, any prominent people, have been brought in today."

Larry raised his eyebrow. "You mean like a certain business man who happens to be on Georgetown's city council?" He leaned his head towards a back room. "There might be someone here that meets that description. Baldwin and Moses brought him in this morning. He was none too happy. It's a shame though if he had anything to do with that girl. She was pretty and way too young."

Just like that Larry confirmed what I needed to know. "What time did they bring him in?"

Larry glanced at his watch, "About an hour ago. The man showed up here with his lawyer."

"Wow, a lawyer already. I sure would like to know if he has a decent alibi."

Before I could coax anything else out of Larry, noise behind me caused me to turn around.

Judith Peters entered the station. By her side was a tall man with a streak of gray running through his dark hair. I'd never seen him before, but the expensive gray suit said lawyer to me. I wondered if Judith was asked to come down to the police station.

Surely, she has an alibi.

I must have been staring way too hard. Suddenly, I found myself facing off with Judith.

Her brown eyes focused sharply on me. "What are you doing here? Haven't you done enough damage to my family?"

I frowned. *What?* It took me a few seconds to gain my composure. "Excuse me. I was hired to do a job by your lawyer. What exactly do you mean haven't I done enough? You received what you asked for from the assignment."

Emotions warred on Judith's face. Her voice sounded strained, "You went too far. When you saw her, you should've just walked away."

I raised my eyebrows. Words wouldn't even come. How could I have a comeback for that? I could understand her regret but blaming me for taking photos she ordered... I gulped, trying to keep my composure. "You do know your husband, or soon to be ex-husband, could be the blame here, right? Are you defending him now? Someone killed Samantha."

"I think that's enough, ladies." When the man who stood by Judith finally spoke, his eyes bored into me. "Mrs. Peters is obviously upset about the loss of Samantha. She wants the person found who did this."

Judith turned from me as if deciding she no longer wanted to acknowledge my existence.

I was still contemplating her burst of anger when a door opened down the hall. Detective Moses stepped out of the room followed by Detective Baldwin. Both men looked exhausted. I wondered if either of them slept last night. They were in for a long day.

I peeked around them hoping to see the person they interrogated.

Edwin Peters stepped out, shrugging into his overcoat. A shorter man with a balding head walked beside him. His lawyer, I assumed.

I stared at Edwin, observing the bright red scar on his face. The very same scratch that Samantha had given him two nights before. His face was smug and didn't seem to be the least bit remorseful or even grief-stricken, which made him appear just plain guilty.

But why was Edwin walking out of the police station? Surely they could hold the man on something. I knew they could hold him for at least seventy-two hours. The man's alibi may have been tight enough that they couldn't arrest him, but even I knew there was evidence of assault on Samantha's body. Surely they could link Edwin's DNA.

Moses caught my attention as I stared at Edwin. He looked like he wanted to question me, but a scuffle soon had all our attention.

Quicker than anyone would have assumed, Judith was in front of Edwin shouting, "How could you do this to us?"

I hadn't noticed how huge Judith's purse was until I saw it collide with Edwin's head. The man was tall and stocky, but the blow had him stumbling backwards.

Judith shrieked as if she was a madwoman. Baldwin and her lawyer attempted to grab her arms and stop her from assaulting her contemptuous husband.

A part of me wanted to jump and lay a lick on him myself, but I continued observing from where I stood. I don't know how much time passed by, but Judith was eventually sequestered inside the interview room and an extra bruised Edwin was escorted out the building. I'm pretty sure there would be others who would want to beat on the man.

"Why are you here, Rena?"

I turned to see Moses staring me down. I smiled back. Moses and I were actually decent friends despite his bad cop routine on me. I didn't much like him when I was the lead eyewitness on another case last year. But his gruffness grew on me when I realized how much of a father figure he was to my godson, Chris. Moses dated my godson's mom, Alecia, and I knew how protective he was of both of them.

I crossed my arms, "To catch the action of course. I'm glad I got a ringside seat." I raised my eyebrow. "Whose idea was it to time that altercation?"

Moses rolled his eyes. "No one expected that to happen. We were happy to talk with both of them away from each other."

As he walked away, I followed. "So both are suspects? Are you leaning towards one or the other?"

Moses ignored me and poured himself a coffee. He had broad shoulders that were currently sagging as if he hadn't slept in days. He turned around. "Once again, I will ask, why are you here?"

"Because I can't get Samantha out of my mind. I was the one who called 9-1-1. She could have easily been strangled to death with her crime scene in another jurisdiction." I bit my lip and then added. "I feel like I should have stayed longer and tried to get her to talk."

Moses' ornery face slipped to one of concern. "You did what you could, Rena. Obviously, the crime scene could have been in a different place if it wasn't for you."

"So Edwin Peters has an alibi for the timeline of Samantha's death?"

Moses stared at his mug. "Let's just say we're still squaring away the facts. He claimed he hadn't left

Pawleys Island until yesterday morning. He was busy all day, in and out of meetings. It's looking hard to pin him showing up to Samantha's house to confront her on Wednesday night."

I folded my arms, "I want to see the crime scene."

Moses' eyes widened. "Why would you want to do that to yourself?"

"Someone showed up after I left her. I want to get inside her world, her last hours."

He vehemently shook his head. "No. You don't need to see the crime scene."

I asked, "Photos?"

Moses looked away.

"Come on, Moses." I wasn't too proud to beg. I really wanted to know.

Moses sighed, "She was a pretty girl. I've seen her photos on social media. There was so much life in her smile. So young."

I dropped my head. "I've seen her Instagram photos too."

"Good, keep those images in your head."

I lifted my head to look at him, "You're stubborn. The coroner had to see the bruises around her neck."

Moses closed his eyes, "Yes, the bruises are visible. It could have been assumed that she was strangled. It was good to get a timeline of what happened at Pawleys Island."

"You've got to get Edwin Peters."

Moses looked at me as if I'd lost my mind. "We can't tie Edwin to her death if he wasn't there."

I swallowed as anger bubbled inside me. Maybe it was good Moses wouldn't let me see the photos. I might have become unhinged from the sight. I liked to think of myself as a tough woman, but in actuality, I was more bark than bite. My curt attitude had been my defense mechanism all my life.

"Can I ask one more question?"

Moses sighed deeply as if in pain. "I couldn't stop you if I wanted to. Ask away, Rena."

"How do you know someone else was there? Suppose she just fell?"

His eyes glazed over, focusing beyond me. "The living room was a mess. A chair had been tipped over, the coffee table was flipped over and whatever was on top, bills, magazines… were strewn across the carpet." He held out his arms. "The altercation moved back towards the kitchen. A bottle of red wine was smashed on the tile floor. At first glance, it looked like blood, but there was no blood visible on the victim. It was like someone pushed her, but she could have tripped. There was a welt on her forehead, so it's likely that she smacked her head against the stove when she went down. The impact must have snapped her neck."

I crossed my arms, picturing the scenario in my head. "A strong person?"

Moses' eyes focused on me. "Or a really angry person…"

There was at least two persons of interest that I knew of. "Was there anything under Samantha's nails? Surely she fought back to defend herself."

"What the coroner found may go back to her altercation with Edwin. We made notes and took pictures of the scratch on his face. We also asked him to provide DNA. Any fibers the team picked off the victim were sent the lab, but it'll be a few weeks. We still need to know who else could have visited Samantha."

He'd placed his hands on my arm as if to guide me out of the police station. "Look, I need to join Baldwin in the interview with Mrs. Peters." He gave me a look. "I'm sure you did what you needed to do to support Mrs. Peters' divorce, but this murder investigation doesn't need to be your concern. We have it, Rena."

I watched Moses as he walked away. He might have thought he dismissed me, but I had no intentions of letting go of what and who happened to Samantha Livingston. The girl had to defend herself from whoever she trusted enough to let into her apartment. Or someone she trusted enough to have access to her apartment. It hurt me deeply to know how she died after escaping Edwin. Did she truly escape?

I waved to Deputy Wilson on my way out and pulled out my phone, seeking a response that I hoped appeared soon. I needed face-to-face access to someone close to Samantha. Janine Peters wasn't an option. At least not yet. But I'd received my wish.

Amir Wright had responded back to my message. One of the first things I decided to do before coming to the station was reach out to Amir via Facebook messenger.

I also had to send a friend request. Facebook rules for engaging were just plain weird. According to the message, it had taken him almost two hours to respond.

He wanted to meet, and I was thrilled to get an inside view of Samantha from someone who really knew her.

Someone who wasn't bad to look at either.

For a brief moment, I wondered if he was also on Baldwin and Moses' list of people to interview.

Chapter Ten

Friday, 12:12 pm

Amir was indeed a beautiful man. Despite my gawking at him last night on social media, that experience did little to prepare me for meeting him in person. I had to remind myself not to forget to breathe as I reached out to shake his hand. He was gracious enough to meet me at Starbucks on what I assumed what his lunch break. Dressed in a navy blue suit underneath a crisp white shirt accented by a slim red tie, the man caused my heart to palpitate.

For some reason, looking at all the photos of the casually dressed, sometimes shirtless man, it hadn't occurred to me that he was a professional.

I blinked, trying to focus my attention. "Thank you for meeting me, Mr. Wright."

He smiled slightly, causing his dimples to appear. "Not a problem. Call me Amir."

I slipped into the booth that he'd found before I arrived. Thankful for the opportunity to save my wobbly knees. *The man has dimples, my kryptonite.* "I'm assuming you are on your lunch break so I will make this brief."

His smile disappeared as he took a sip of his coffee. "I do have a meeting this afternoon, but we have time. You wanted to ask me about Samantha. Did you say you were a private investigator?"

"Yes, I am. I was doing work for a client when I ran across Samantha the other night." I cleared my throat. This wasn't an easy conversation to just break into since I didn't know how much this young man knew.

He frowned, "The other night? You mean the night she died?"

That surprised me. "Yes, I saw her on Wednesday, early evening. Did you two talk on Wednesday?"

Amir's shoulders slumped. "Samantha and I talked pretty much every other night. At least two or three times a week. Sometimes we met each other for dinner. She and I have been friends forever. Really, she was like my little sister."

"But you didn't see her Wednesday night?"

He winced. "No, I wished I had. She called me, and I could tell she was upset. When I returned her call, she sounded like she was driving in her car. She wouldn't tell me what was bothering her. I offered to come over, but she told me no. I felt guilty about not going to see her anyway so I called her the next morning. In fact, I left several messages all day yesterday. I finally just left work a bit early and swung by her place."

"So, you found her?"

He stared out the window, pain flashing in his eyes. "I did. I wish I hadn't seen her like that. I can't get the image of her lying there on the floor out of my mind. It didn't seem real."

I watched Amir clench his fists. He let out a deep breath and wiped at his eyes before turning back to me. "Can I ask why you really want to talk to me?"

His candor took me aback, but it shouldn't have. His friend had just died and here I was questioning him. "I wanted to know more about Samantha. If there's anything I can do..."

He interrupted, "Like what? You can't bring her back."

"I'm sorry. No, but I can help find out who did this. I was a reporter in Charlotte for many years. I know how to search for things."

He frowned, "Why not let the cops handle it?"

I leaned in, "Did the cops question you yesterday? You know they always look pretty closely at the person who found the victim?"

He flinched. "They asked me some questions, but I was at work all day. I hadn't seen her since the weekend. Like I said, when I called, I could tell she was shook up. I was a bit concerned that she was driving upset. I knew she'd gone to see Edwin Peters. She wouldn't confirm, but I figured he'd upset her."

Now that did surprise me. "So, did Samantha tell you why she was going to see Mr. Peters? The man was her best friend's dad."

Amir looked out the window as if something outside was more interesting than my question. When he finally turned to me, his eyes were stormy and teeming with pain. "I'm pretty sure Samantha went to see Edwin for the same reason she usually did."

Amir was being vague, and I didn't want to rock the boat. But I needed him to tell me more. I thought for a moment about Samantha's social media. She had to spend a lot of money on clothes and makeup. I ventured a guess, "Edwin Peters is a wealthy businessman. Did Samantha reach out to him for money sometimes?"

He cringed, "Samantha wasn't very good with handling her finances. She was probably late on her rent again."

I watched as Amir gripped his hands into fists.

"I told her to stop going to him. If she needed help, she could ask me. She always went into this downward spiral emotionally after she asked for money. She would never tell me why, but I figured there was something to the exchange. I didn't want to upset her."

I hoped my face didn't reflect what I saw last night. So this wasn't the first time Samantha reached out to Edwin. Maybe her slap to his face was born of frustration and anger. Amir was only aware that she went to Edwin for money. I imagined he would be crushed if he knew something more was involved.

I steered the questions in a different direction. "Can you tell me how you met Samantha? You said you knew her forever."

He leaned back in the booth, unclenching his fists as if just realizing he needed to relax. "Sam, that's what I call her. We were in the same foster home for a while."

"Foster home? I heard Samantha's mother died when she young."

"Yeah, when she was ten. Sam bounced around foster homes for a while until her grandmother was able to take her in. Then her grandmother got sick."

"Didn't she live with the Peters for a while too?"

Amir narrowed his eyes. "You've really done your homework."

I shrugged. "Mrs. Peters mentioned it in a conversation yesterday."

"Samantha loved Judith like she was her own mom. Janine and her are … were tight like sisters." Amir's hands clenched again. "You know, now that I think about it, one time Sam mentioned he wanted her to run some errands for him."

Errands. I wondered what type of errand. What had he asked her to do?

Amir stared down at the table, a man who'd truly lost his best friend.

I wanted to change the tone of the conversation before I lost Amir into his obvious grief. "So, what was Samantha's usual personality?"

He smiled, "She was mainly positive. She loved clothes and makeup. Man, that girl spent tons of time and money shopping. I used to tell her she should concentrate on her education. If she wanted to go to college, the Peters would have helped her, but she didn't. She got a job at that salon and that's where she's been since she was eighteen."

I opened up my notebook and peered at my notes. "She worked at Essence Beauty Salon?"

"Yeah, she was good at what she did. She liked making women feel good about themselves." Amir's face crumpled, and for a minute, it looked like he wouldn't be able to keep his composure. Finally, he choked out, "I wish she was more secure about herself."

Without realizing it, I'd reached out and touched Amir's right hand which was still clenched. He let out a slow breath and I felt his hand relax.

I snatched my hand back, suddenly feeling my heated face.

Why in the world did you do that? The past me would have never felt this self-conscious about being around a man.

I gulped, hoping to contain my discomfort. "I'm really sorry about your loss. Samantha sounds like she was an amazing woman. I'm going to do all I can to assist the police investigation. Do you know if Samantha had any enemies?"

He looked at me. "I want to say no that everyone loved her, but Samantha ... was a pretty girl. She caught the attention of guys all the time, and she had some run-ins with jealous women. I can't say anyone outright hated her though. Not to do this." His face crumpled again. "She was on the floor. I knew something was wrong because she was so still."

"Did you have a key?"

He sucked in a breath and wiped his face. "Yes, the apartment was mine first. We were roommates until I found a new place." He chuckled. "It was getting awkward with us trying to have a friend over... romantically."

His comment made me blush. Regaining my composure, I started to inquire more about his access to the apartment when I felt someone staring at me. I swiveled my head to the right to find Trey watching me. His gaze drifted to Amir and then back to me.

Suddenly, my actions a minute ago haunted me. How long had Trey been here and had he seen me reach over to touch Amir's hand?

Perfect timing. I'm sure he got the wrong impression.

Chapter Eleven

Friday, 1:03 pm

Why was it when I tried to avoid a man, I couldn't shake him? Not that I totally wanted to avoid Trey. But this was awkward. I did the only thing I could do, I grinned and waved at Trey. Cringing inside, I thought, *I guess it's time to wrap this meeting up.* All the gawking I'd been doing, Trey probably noticed that too.

I reached into my purse and pulled out one of my cards. I handed the card to Amir. "I really don't want to hold you up, and I know this is really raw for you right now. Maybe we can catch up again if you think of anything else."

Amir peered over his shoulder to see who had caught my attention. When he turned back, the impish grin on his face made me squirm. He slowly took the card from my hand. "Boyfriend?"

I swallowed. Hard. I had to recover from Amir's fingers touching mine. The man was electric.

"Um, no, just a really good friend. We've known each other forever … kind of like you and Samantha." I cleared my throat, "Enough about me. I hope we can touch base again. I may have a few more questions."

86

He slipped my card into his inside coat pocket. "Sure, I'm still in shock. I probably shouldn't have worked today, but this afternoon's meeting was pretty important." He stood and reached out his hand to me. "It was good talking you, Ms. Manchester."

I smiled and shook his hand. *Firm grip, soft hands.* "Rena is fine."

"Rena, I like that." His eyes were transfixed on me.

Though I knew Trey was nearby, I couldn't look away from Amir.

He broke whatever strange trance was going on between us. "By the way, I'm working on arrangements for Samantha. After today's meeting, I will be more focused on her final wishes. I'm planning her funeral for Monday."

"Wow, that has to be hard."

He grimaced, "I know what she wanted, and she was the closest person I ever had as family. If it was me, she would do the same. Neither one of us have family. Or at least reliable family."

I nodded, "I plan to be there."

"Thank you."

I watched as Amir left before turning my attention to Trey, who approached me with weariness in his eyes. Or was that something else?

He was the last person I expected to bump into at Starbucks. "Hey, you. This is a surprise. I thought you didn't care for Starbucks. Have a seat."

Trey slid into the booth; his face had gone blank to hide whatever was going on inside. "I don't usually, but I thought I saw your car."

That made me raise an eyebrow. I didn't have one of those cars that stood out. My Honda Civic was a pretty ordinary car. I saw cars like mine all the time, especially when I couldn't seem to recall where I parked my own car in a massive lot.

He looked at my face and then cracked a grin. "Really, I wasn't stalking you. I have office supplies in my car to prove that I was just over at Staples."

His grin was contagious, so I grinned back. "It's good to see you. I thought you were going to call last night about getting together."

"I started too, but I thought you'd want a break after yesterday morning."

I peered down and then back up. "Yesterday was a bit awkward."

He flashed the dimples I'd fallen in love with as preteen, appearing sheepish.

I definitely had a thing for men with dimples.

His response was so low, and I had to lean closer to hear him.

"I guess that's my fault for forcing you to do breakfast."

I rolled my eyes, "Please, you can't force me to do anything. That free will thing God gave us."

Trey chuckled, but then his face grew serious. "Was the guy sitting here before me the reason you're not wanting to take our relationship any further?"

For a brief instance, I felt confused.

What in the world was he talking about?

"You mean Amir? No, I just met him today. His friend was killed Wednesday night, and I happened to be on an assignment for Clay. It's crazy, but I saw she was in trouble and called 9-1-1 to help her." I took a deep breath not realizing how much this was really getting to me. "Then, I found out the next day from Moses and Baldwin that she'd been killed."

Trey took my hand. "I'm sorry, Rena. I didn't know all this was happening. So, are you still on an assignment for Clay? He's mainly a divorce attorney, right?"

I nodded, "Yeah, but his client and her soon to be ex-husband are tied to the victim."

Trey raised an eyebrow. "I see. Still sounds like a murder investigation for the police."

"Believe me, Baldwin and Moses have let me know that... even after I helped them last year."

Trey sighed. His own son was caught up in that same case. Joseph's mom was dating an ex-con who had all kinds of danger brewing around him. Poor Joseph almost got hurt.

"Still, you and Joseph could've gotten hurt last year. I know you've been chomping at the bit to get a different kind of case, just be careful."

"I am. You saw I met the guy in a very public place." I narrowed my eyes. "I've been investigating dirt on all kinds of people most of my life. It's what I did all those years in Charlotte, Trey. This isn't new to me."

Trey licked his lips like he was pondering what to say next. Due to the fact that he was a bit predictable like my sister, I could guess what he was going to say.

I held up my hand to stop him. "Please, don't act like Bev on this one. I know my getting hurt a few years back caused me to lose my career and end up back home. Just because I'm in Georgetown doesn't me I'm going to give up on what I'm good at doing."

"No one is asking you to do that, Rena."

"Good."

His smile returned, though the concern in his eyes continued to bore into me. "I'm glad I ran into you. Joseph will be staying at the house this weekend. He asked about you. Maybe you can swing by tomorrow for that dinner we talked about."

I nodded. "Well, since Joseph will be there."

He laughed softly, "Since you seem to feel like we need to take things slow, a sixteen-year-old boy should definitely take care of that."

I laughed. "I'll be there."

"Good, see you about three o'clock."

Trey slid from the seat. Before he walked away, he placed his hand on my shoulder. The warmth of his squeeze drew more comfort than I expected. I watched him walk out, admiring his mature profile.

While Trey was joking about having his son around, I was relieved. Being alone around Trey was not good for my psyche. I'd been on this unintended celibacy kick for three years, which started with my injury and then when I really learned about Jesus for myself, I realized how easily I let the wrong men into my life. I also began to see how my dad and stepdad influenced some of my bad decisions over the years. These were two men that had disappointed me to my core, and in many ways, I was still healing.

Despite my strict upbringing under my stepdad, Reverend Lawson, I'd avoided church most of my adult life. During my healing process from the head injury, I discovered there was a whole lot more to Christianity. Running away from religion all those years had also caused me to miss the opportunity to develop a relationship with God.

While I prayed about my struggles, I still wasn't understanding how to balance my relationship with God with my growing desire to be with the long-lost love of my youth. I'd already been married twice in my lifetime, and those two disastrous marriages hung over me.

Did I even have it in me to be a wife?

Today, it appeared I seemed to be having trouble keeping my hands off a good looking, young man with dimples. My earlier impulse to reach out to Amir still gnawed at me.

Did Trey see that?

He had to know I wasn't meant to be more than a friend to him. Ever. I was, and had always been, a woman who came with bad baggage.

My coffee had long since gone cold, but I downed the rest of it before leaving Starbucks. The coffeehouse was like a second home to me during my reporter days. I had to admit it felt satisfying to be investigating something different. I just hated that a young woman lost her life.

It was still early in the afternoon, and I had one more stop to make before I would call it a day. Thankfully, the next man on my list disgusted me too much to even be remotely interested in him. I just wanted to see him go down for something.

Chapter Twelve

Friday, 4:13 pm

I sat around for almost fifteen minutes at Waterway Commercial Real Estate before I could see Edwin Peters. The man didn't come from old money, but he knew how to bring in money from some big commercial real estate dealings. From my research, Edwin specialized in selling coastal properties and land along the South Carolina coast from Myrtle Beach to Hilton Head. His office was located in a building that seemed modern on the outside, but when I entered, there were remnants of the past.

One of those being Edwin's secretary. The nameplate on her desk was stamped Irma Brown. The woman, who appeared to be in her late fifties or early sixties, kept eyeing me over her reading glasses. Her hair was an unnatural platinum blonde and seemed to be stiff with hairspray. As many times as I observed her, her hair never moved. It remained curled around her head in a halo of curls. Her green eyes were sharp and piercing as if she could will me to leave the office if she wanted me to.

I had no intentions of going anywhere. I'd been tailing Edwin for a week until I finally caught him two nights ago with Samantha. Now, I wanted a personal conversation with him. Amir's mention of Samantha running errands in exchange for money had me thinking of all kinds of scenarios. None of them good.

Alibi or no alibi, I wanted to get a sense of whether or not Edwin was the kind of person to get someone else to do his dirty work for him. He may have never set foot in Samantha's apartment, but the man had the money to pay someone to kill her. Every angle had to be investigated. While I'm sure Baldwin and Moses were doing their jobs, I needed to be sure for myself.

Finally, Edwin's door opened. Irma stood and glided over to the door, peering in.

I heard her murmur something, and Edwin's rough voice floated out the door. Irma flinched before stepping away from the door. She looked at me with something like pity in her eyes. I couldn't tell if the pity was for me or herself for having to work for the man.

"You can go in now." Irma's voice was hoarse.

I gave her a slight nod, "Thank you." I suspected Irma smoked several packs a day. As I passed by her desk, I saw her reach for a pack in her desk drawer.

Apparently, she was taking this time to grab a smoke break. My dad was a smoker. I never understood what people got out of that little white stick of death.

I walked to Edwin's open door and knocked.

He answered without looking up. "Come in."

What struck me as I walked into Edwin's office was how pristine it looked. He sat behind a large mahogany desk. The walls were lined with large bookcases on each side. Like his secretary's hair, Edwin's office reminded me of another era. Even though the building appeared modern on the outside, the furniture was from the eighties. It was clean with no visible signs of dust, but it felt ancient.

Judith was the one from old money. Her family's legacy could be traced back to when this area was nothing but rice fields and plantations. The very land Edwin made it his business to sell.

As I stepped into the office, Edwin looked up. I almost flinched as my eyes landed on the scar on Edwin's cheek. The cause of that scar was a remnant of Samantha's struggle to fight back, but it wasn't much of a fair fight. Edwin was a huge man, pudgy in areas from age and probably sitting in this office too much. His large hands around Samantha's throat dragging her small frame still haunted me.

Now that I was in his presence, I questioned if it was smart of me to approach him like this.

He eyed me with interest. I imagined he was a man who mainly looked at a woman for her body first. If he looked at a woman for anything more, I would be surprised.

I wore my usual uniform, sweatshirt and jeans. Today, I wore my "fight like a girl" sweatshirt. The pink letters popped against the brown shirt. The slogan was for women fighting breast cancer, but I'm sure Edwin would interpret it his own way. My back stiffened as I held out my hand, "Thank you for seeing me, Mr. Peters."

He stood as I approached, but he didn't reach out to shake my hand. "My secretary says you're a private detective. For who?"

I dropped my hand to the side, thankful that I didn't have to touch his hand. The act of touching him may have had me running out of the office. Knowing I was on shaky ground here, I needed to tread carefully. I wasn't here investigating on behalf of Clay. If anything, I was here under my own detective license for my own personal reasons.

"Can't say. Client confidentiality. I hope you won't mind if I ask you a few questions? I will be out of your hair in no time."

Not that he had much hair. At the phase where he should just shave his head entirely, Edwin was balding badly. But the man didn't have a perfect round head, so I could imagine why he held onto the hair he had.

He peeked at the large gold watch on his wrist. "Have a seat, Ms. Manchester. I have a few minutes." He leaned back in his chair, tipping it backwards a bit.

I sat in the leather chair in front of his desk. While it appeared stiff, I felt my bottom sank into the seat. I leaned forward so I could remain more perched on the edge. "I'm looking into the death of Samantha Livingston. I understand you knew her."

His eyes narrowed, "You are a private detective and not a reporter?"

I'd given Irma my card when I arrived. I peered down at his desk and noticed my business card in front of him. I pointed, "Yes, that business card is legitimate." He didn't need to know I was a reporter in a past life.

"Why are you looking into Samantha's death? That's for the police."

I smiled. "Sometimes I can find out details the police wouldn't be able to find." Anxious to get something out of the man, I asked. "How long have you known her?"

He winced, "I guess since she was a little girl. She's my daughter's best friend. After her mom died, she lived with us."

I thought of my earlier conversation with Amir. "Was this after she was in foster care?"

He paused before answering, "After her mother died, Samantha was in foster care for maybe a year. Her grandmother raised her for a brief time until she grew ill. Samantha started living with us when she turned fourteen."

I recalled Judith's reaction to Samantha's mom. "Did you know Samantha's mom?"

Edwin fiddled with his tie, not meeting my eyes. "Yes, I knew Tabitha growing up." He added, "She was my best friend's wife."

His best friend's wife. So Edwin knew Samantha's parents. For some reason, his dealing with the young woman made my blood boil even more.

"Tabitha, you said her name was. She died when Samantha was young?"

"Yes, my friend, Samantha's dad, Bruce Livingston, was killed in Afghanistan. His death was really hard on Tabitha. All of us really. Tabitha was always a bit of a wild girl. She started drinking and then moved on to other stuff after Bruce died."

"That was good of you to take Samantha in."

He nodded, "It was the right thing to do after losing Bruce and Tabitha. Taking care of their little girl was the least I could do."

I decided to switch up. Edwin was trying to paint himself as a do-gooder, and I knew he wasn't. "Samantha was very popular online. I'm wondering if she attracted some unnecessary attention. She seemed to have an endless income to be able to buy clothes and makeup. Do you know if she had any debts?"

Edwin sat forward suddenly, causing his chair to squeak. "She liked nice things. So does my daughter, but I'm not aware of any debts. Do you think some scumbag online did this?"

"She was a pretty girl and very popular," I didn't miss a beat. "Since she was a part of your family, maybe you helped Samantha buy these nice things. It certainly seemed like she couldn't afford the name brand designers from her earnings at the salon."

His eyes narrowed. "Samantha was like a daughter to me. We helped her out."

"I'm sure Samantha was grateful. I'm curious, did Samantha look like her mother?"

Something passed over Edwin's face that seemed to resemble regret. Or was he reminiscing? A theory entered my mind, and I forced it back so I could hear his response.

After a moment, Edwin smiled. "Samantha was Tabitha's mini-me."

Something about Edwin's smile made my skin crawl. "Oh, I see."

I was one of those people who wasn't good at hiding facial reactions. There must have been something on my face; Edwin's eyes flashed in anger and his cheeks turned red. "Why are you really here?" he boomed. "The police wanted to pin this on me. Well, they can't. I was nowhere near Samantha's place. I don't know who killed her."

"But I heard you did try to harm her." Heard, I actually saw, but I wasn't going to let Edwin know I was the person behind the camera.

He jumped up from his chair, causing me to spring from chair where I sat. "Get out. You don't know what you're talking about."

I inched my way back towards the door. "Are you saying you didn't try to harm Samantha the night before she died? Maybe you lost it in a fit of emotion?"

He stepped from behind the desk. Edwin had a temper, but I wasn't ready to leave yet.

"I did NOT kill Samantha. My alibi is solid. I better not see you anywhere near my business or my family, Ms. Manchester. I don't know what you think you're doing, but your investigation stops now."

Not a chance. I'm just getting started.

I made my way to the open door. "Thank you for your time, Mr. Peters. I only want to know more about Samantha and who could have done this. I wasn't accusing you of anything."

I turned and marched out the office. With a side glance, I noticed Irma had returned to her desk. Her eyes were wide. Almost fearful. I guess it wasn't going to be a good afternoon for her since I upset her boss.

Clay's statement about Edwin's finances being more than what they appeared on paper struck a chord with me. I was still working for Clay, and whether

Judith wanted me to dig up more on her husband or not, she was paying Clay to win big on the divorce settlement.

After I climbed into my car, I looked at the two-story building. Someone stood at the second floor window peering at me. I couldn't make out the facial features, but the shape of the figure was large enough to let me know it was probably Edwin. Him watching me encouraged me to turn the key in the engine. I needed to get out of here.

As I drove, the theory that started to form in his office took shape in my mind. I suspected Edwin had a thing for Tabitha, his best friend's wife that somehow spilled onto the daughter. I don't know when it started, but at some point Edwin took advantage of Samantha's need for money. Her best friend, Amir was concerned and seemed unaware of how ugly the situation had become. Judith was surprised, and with the revelation, her anger went back to Samantha's mother. Yesterday, Judith's despise of Samantha's mother was obvious as she spoke about the woman.

Did she know her husband had feelings for Tabitha? Of course she did. If so, how could she not have missed the signs of those past feelings spilling over to the daughter?

And how was Janine reacting to all of this? Did she know what her father had done? Did either mother or daughter have a sense or were their heads under a rock?

In all of the adulterous affairs I'd caught on my camera in the past months as a private investigator, this case went up another notch in the creepy category. I couldn't get home fast enough. I needed a shower. As I glanced at my reflection in the mirror, another thought started to brew.

I could use some pampering too.

Chapter Thirteen

Saturday, November 10, 10:02 am

Back during my days in Charlotte, I had a regular appointment with the most fabulous hair stylist. I didn't realize how much I missed him until I walked into Essence Beauty Salon. It was definitely a busy Saturday morning. I could see stylists lined up on both sides as soon as I walked in. The salon had a classy interior with a black and white decor. The stylists were all dressed in black tops and pants. A young girl who was probably Samantha's age greeted me at the receptionist area. I guessed from her red-rimmed eyes she may have been grieving.

Next to her stood a man who immediately captured my attention. He was tall, with smooth ebony skin. His wore dreadlocks pulled back in a ponytail that hung down his back. Dressed in a fitted black t-shirt and black jeans, I wasn't sure whether he was a part of the staff or not. He was a beautiful man. This was turning out to be the most interesting week I've had in a while when it came to males. I would be spending the afternoon with Trey and Joseph.

Behind me, two women bustled in, both complaining about the rainy weather outside. I stepped to the side so they could check in with the receptionist. I assumed both were sisters since they appeared to be so much alike. Both wore glasses and were dressed in tracksuits. It seemed like I'd seen both around town before, maybe even at church. While I'd been back home a year, sometimes I felt like a stranger in the small town where I grew up.

One of the women whined, "Zeke, this weather is horrible. You going to get me all fixed up, and then I have to deal with buckets of rain."

The other woman piped in, "We should have scheduled for yesterday."

Zeke smiled and his perfectly set white teeth seemed to brighten the room. "Ladies, you know I will take care of you. Let us do our magic and don't worry about the rain outside."

I watched as he ushered the two women to the back. The young woman behind the counter looked at me expectantly. "Ma'am, do you have an appointment?"

"No, I don't. Do you accept walk-ins?"

She looked at my hair which I had pulled up into a puff on the top of my head. "Depends on what you want done."

"How about a wash and some simple flat-twists."

She looked at the calendar. "Zeke may be able to fit you in. I need to ask him."

"Sure." I waited at the counter for the girl to return. She returned with Zeke following behind her. He met my eyes with a friendly smile. "What can I do for you, pretty lady?"

I found myself blushing, something I didn't normally do. "Well, I haven't been to a salon in a really long time. I've been natural for about two years. Think you can give me something different?"

He examined my hair from where he stood. "We can hook you up. You need to show off your crown and that pretty face of yours. Give your info to Cherry here and she will bring you back."

I smiled. "Sure. My name is Serena Manchester or you can just put Rena. It's what most people call me."

The girl jotted down my name and contact info. Soon, I was whisked to the back, covered in a cape and seated in a chair in front of a large porcelain black sink. My hair was washed and scalp stroked with Zeke's strong fingers. The shampoo smelled like coconuts and brought me visions of being on some tropical island.

It wasn't until I was seated in a styling chair and peered over at a booth that I was jolted back into the reason why I came to the salon. The booth next to me was dark and on the counter was a framed photo of Samantha. Next to the photo were several flowers and cards.

Zeke had finished blow drying my hair and seemed to noticed my attentiveness to the display. His eyes were sad. "We lost a member of our staff this week. We're all brokenhearted and wasn't sure what else to do."

That was my cue. "Samantha?"

He gazed at me in surprise, and then narrowed his eyes but continued to part my hair. "Yes, did you know her?"

"No, but I've learned a lot about her the past few days."

Zeke held up his hand as if he wasn't sure if he should continue.

I realized I made a mistake having someone work on my hair while trying to ask them sensitive questions. I took a deep breath. "I'm not a reporter, but I am a private investigator. I saw Samantha was in trouble a few nights ago. She was scared and I felt like there was something more I could have done if I'd known what scared her."

Zeke visibly relaxed and continued to work on my hair.

My nervousness didn't disappear though. I hadn't let anyone touch my hair since going natural. After a few moments of silence, Zeke finally spoke. "I don't know if she was scared, but something had been bothering Samantha for weeks. I assumed it was money. She wanted to get more work and I told her that wasn't possible. There was only so much hair we could manage in this shop."

"I heard she had a money source."

Zeke stilled again, only for a moment, then continued flat-twisting my hair.

"If you're talking about her friend's dad, yes, he seemed to like to make sure she was taken care of. Bit of a creep if you asked me."

I met his eyes in the mirror, "I agree with you."

Zeke nodded. "You know he and Samantha's mom were a thing back in the day."

I wasn't surprised, but it was interesting how Zeke let that slip out. I was merely a stranger to him.

"I spoke to Mr. Peters yesterday. He mentioned Tabitha. So you knew her mom?"

Zeke's smile was smug. "Of course. Tabitha was my younger sister's best friend. I thought after Tabitha married and had Samantha that she would calm down a bit. She did for a while, but when her husband died, she went back to her old ways. I believe she reached out to Edwin herself, a time or two."

Zeke caught my eye, "She was involved with Edwin during high school. So they were close enough for her to feel comfortable reaching out to him. My sister would know more about it. It used to frustrate her to see Tabitha go to Edwin. It made us all angry when we saw Samantha doing the same thing."

I blew out a breath. I didn't want to taint Samantha's memory and I didn't know how much people knew about what I witnessed the other night. Still I had to ask. "Do you know why she felt led to go to him?"

Zeke had finished my hair which I had to say looked better than I could have imagined. He passed me the mirror for my inspection before answering my question.

I peered at the back and was thoroughly impressed. "It's beautiful. Thank you."

"Beautiful hairstyle for a beautiful woman." His smile disappeared. "To answer your question, Samantha didn't like having to go to Peters for money. Like I said, if she could earn it herself, she tried to do it. But like most struggling working folks, things happen. She didn't find herself in a bind often, but when she did, she went the easy route. She asked for the money, but I'm sure she paid a price for it."

I recalled Amir mentioning Samantha's errands. "How can you be sure?"

"Because she changed. She was always a positive kid. Always smiling, joy radiated from her. When she went for help, she came back different. Quiet, depressed, staying to herself. I was scared one time that she reverted to drugs or something like her mom, but she hadn't. Still, I know she felt ashamed about something."

I nodded. My mind went back to the night Samantha left Edwin's house. She'd held her head in shame. When I approached her at her apartment, she was scared and ashamed that I caught her with Edwin. I realized at that moment how much guilt the young woman carried. How devastated she would have felt if Judith and Janine found out.

Anger swept over me at how Edwin took advantage of her.

I looked at Zeke who was observing me with interest. "You knew Samantha's mom. Did they look like each other?"

Zeke lifted his chin and narrowed his eyes. "Samantha was the spitting image of her mother. I suspect that's why Edwin took special care of her. I also had other suspicions, but I didn't want to embarrass Samantha. She was a proud girl. She enjoyed what she did on social media. Loved to dress-up and look pretty. She loved to make others feel the same. Samantha was not one to let you see her weakness."

"She hid her pain."

Zeke nodded. "She did that very well. Only the people closest to her would know something was off."

"I know we just met, but would you mind if I reached out to your sister?"

He smiled, "I appreciate someone looking out for Samantha. If my sister," he turned and indicated the other stylists, "or any of us can help find out who did this to Samantha, let us know. I will bring you my sister's phone number."

"Thank you," I whipped out my pocketbook. "It's been a pleasure coming to the salon this morning. I miss this, being pampered. I will be back."

"I hope to see you in here again, pretty lady. You can take care of that up front. Please do schedule another appointment."

"Thank you."

I took care of the bill and made sure to tip Zeke well for his service.

Cherry handed me a folded up piece of paper and looked at me, "Zeke said to give this to you."

"Thank you." I opened the paper to find a name and phone number. Zeke's sister's name was Yvette. I folded the paper back and stuck it in my purse.

Cherry handed me a receipt. "Would you like to make an appointment?"

"Yes, how about in two weeks except not on a Saturday. I prefer a weekday in the morning."

Cherry nodded.

I cleared my throat. "Were you close to Samantha?"

The young woman jerked her head up. "Yes, we've been friends since cosmetology school." Her eyes watered. "I hate this happened. She'd been acting different."

I nudged her, "Scared, maybe? Like someone was bothering her?"

Cherry shook her head and handed me the small card with my next appointment scribbled across the back. "I don't know about scared. Just sad."

"I met her friend Amir. He's planning the funeral for Monday."

A smile crossed Cherry's sad face. "I know, he came by earlier to tell Zeke. Zeke offered to help him. I know this is hard for Amir. Samantha was like his sister."

I recalled from my list that I'd never seen Cherry hanging out with Samantha on social media. I commented, "I guess this is hard for Janine too."

A flash of anger wrestled across Cherry's face. Then she was sad again, but her voice turned indifferent, almost cold. "That family didn't care about her. Especially Janine."

The sharpness of Cherry's tone put me on alert. "I thought they were best friends."

She shrugged, "I guess. Samantha was the better friend. She was a good person..." Tears streamed down her face, dragging mascara with it. She fiercely wiped her tears away. Her eyes pierced me. "Are you going to help find who did this to her?"

"That's my plan."

Cherry looked behind her as if she expected Zeke or one of the other stylists to show up. She leaned forward, "The Peters family had something to do with this. They always brought Samantha down."

The salon door behind me opened and another customer bustled through trying to shut an umbrella as she stepped inside. I nodded at Cherry and stepped outside, lifting the hood of my jacket over my freshly styled hair.

As I jogged towards my car, I couldn't help but think both Zeke and Cherry confirmed my theory about Samantha. Still, it didn't place me any closer to her killer.

All clues pointed to one of the Peters, who on the outside appeared like they really cared for Samantha. But did they really?

Chapter Fourteen

Saturday, 4:57 pm

Between Trey's son, Joseph and my godson, Chris, I'd never spent as much time around two teenage boys. Both of the teens were over at Trey's house enjoying a game of Halo on Joseph's Xbox. They both suckered me into playing until Trey saved me by asking for my assistance in the kitchen. I wasn't doing too well among the whoops and overabundance of young testosterone, so I was more than grateful to escape to the kitchen. I wasn't a cook like Trey, but I was really longing for his company.

The boys' enthusiastic taunts from the living room trailed behind me as I followed Trey to the kitchen. "Thanks for saving me. I've never been much of a gamer."

Trey laughed. "I know they both appreciate you giving it a shot. You mind helping me mash the potatoes?"

I grabbed the potato masher from his hands. "I think I can handle that." I reached for the bowl of now cooled potatoes and began to mash away. It was pretty therapeutic. The morning at Essence Beauty Salon had been a somber experience.

"You seem quiet. Are you okay?" Trey asked.

"I'm just really affected by this week's events."

"You mean the girl who was murdered? Samantha was her name, right? I saw her on the news last night. She seemed to be popular. Who would have imagined a young girl from a small town in South Carolina having that many Instagram followers?"

I grimaced. "Her death is just tragic. She lost her parents when she was young. One to war, the other to a battle with drugs. She had people take her in, but I'm thinking one person really didn't have her best interest in mind."

Trey moved beside me and took the bowl of mashed potatoes away. "I heard Edwin Peters was questioned. Was she close to him and his family?"

I watched as Trey basted more sauce on the ribs he was baking in the oven. "Yes. How did you know that about Edwin Peters? Sounds like you've been paying attention to the town grapevine."

He laughed. "You know any time someone is seen at the police station, that's news to share." Trey pushed the rack with the ribs back inside the stove and closed the door. "It came up at choir practice, of all topics to be talking about."

I had to smile. "Church folks know how to gossip too."

He grinned, "Yeah, I don't know Edwin Peters personally, but I use to work for one of the branches of Waterway. He has offices all over, one in Myrtle Beach,

Beaufort, Charleston and the headquarters here in Georgetown."

I frowned. "How did I not know you worked in real estate?"

He grinned. "I guess there is a lot we don't know about each other."

For a second, my self-consciousness returned, making me aware of how close we were standing in the kitchen. It could have been the heat radiating from the stove, but I took a step towards the refrigerator, thinking there were plenty of things I didn't want Trey to ever know about me. "I'm thirsty, you have some bottled water."

I opened the fridge and stuck my head in, grateful for the coolness. I grabbed a water and turned to see if Trey wanted one. The look he was giving me made me no longer feel the coolness from the refrigerator. I stood up. "Why are you grinning like that?"

Trey shook his head and chuckled softly. "I don't know what to do about you sometimes, Rena." He walked around me and grabbed a six pack of Coke. I'm going to see if the guys want anything to drink. Keep an eye on the oven for me."

"Sure." I placed myself on one of the stools around the kitchen island. By the time Trey returned to the kitchen, my heart rate had slowed considerably.

While he stirred the baked beans, I decided to start the conversation up again, hoping not to get as flustered. "So, how was it working at Waterway? Why did you leave?"

Trey grabbed a dish rag and wiped his hands. "To answer your first question, being at Waterway was exciting at first. Then, I started to see a side of the business I didn't like, and I just grew tired. I was starting to feel called into ministry and looking at attending seminary school, so I applied and was accepted to Dallas Theological Seminary. I've been the minister of music at Zion for almost nine years now. Being at Waterway was a different time in my life. Just a job to carry me until I found out where the Lord wanted me to be."

I nudged, "You said there was a side of the business you didn't like. Explain."

"Well, you know Waterway buys and sells land around the coast of South Carolina. That's big business. There was one time they wanted to acquire land that had been in this family for years. I remember how adamant the older lady was about not selling her land. I felt for her and really didn't want to push her, although it would have done wonders for my status and commission record. A few weeks later, she suddenly passed. Her land was passed to her kids, and all of them signed on the dotted line to sell the land."

"Wow. None of the kids wanted to keep it?"

Trey shook his head. "They all lived outside of South Carolina. It was property they'd grown up on, but none of them were interested in keeping it. There were taxes that had to be paid every year. I thought at the time that was such a shame. I couldn't get the woman out of my mind with how proud she was to pass that land down to her children. It was her legacy."

"So, that happened often?"

Trey shrugged, "Probably too often. It really bothered me that a lot of the land was owned by African

Americans. You know most of us didn't get that forty acre and a mule, but back during Reconstruction, some folks were able to acquire land. That land stayed in the family at least until relatives moved away and the responsibility of paying taxes became a struggle for descendants. It was heartbreaking to see this land snapped up. Anyway, it wasn't a world I missed."

I watched Trey lean down to pull the sizzling ribs from the oven. Without knowing it, Trey had just passed on a lead to help me look a bit deeper into Edwin's finances. If I couldn't connect him to Samantha's death, I was still determined to find something shady about the man. Clay had already hinted that Edwin made his income from more than just real estate dealings. What if some of the properties were acquired in a not so legal manner?

After we devoured the meal, I followed Trey out to the back porch. It was a closed-in back porch with large windows on each side. In the middle was a wood burning stove. Trey bent over to add more wood to the fire.

I sat on an old worn sofa, grabbing the blanket that hung across the back. It was just enough chill in the air, but I could feel the warmth radiating from the stove. It could have been the meal I just ate or the heat, but I was starting to feel sleepy. If my senses were more alert, I would have moved the second I felt Trey sit beside me on the couch. When his arm went around me, I should have tensed, but I didn't.

In all honesty, it felt comforting for him to be beside me.

We sat for a long time, both of us fixated on the burning flames inside the stove.

Trey broke the silence. "I don't want you to run from me, Rena. I'm not going to force anything on you. We've been friends most of our lives, and I'd like to still think of you as my best friend. I want you to know that I'm here for you. You're not alone anymore. There's nothing for you to be ashamed of to feel you have to hide. You are a new creature in Christ. He sees you and accepts you for who you are. He does that for all of us. Don't run from Him. Don't run from me."

Something stuck in my throat. If I wanted to respond, I couldn't. Instead, I closed my eyes. A tear ran down the side of my face, and I felt Trey's warm hand wipe it away. I wrapped the blanket tighter around me and succumbed to the sleep. There was no need to fight it. I knew I was safe in Trey's presence.

Still, I felt unworthy of this man's love.

Chapter Fifteen

Monday, November 12, 2:32 pm

After my Saturday evening with Trey, some of the turmoil that drove me last week subsided. On Sunday, I enjoyed church and dinner with Bev and the girls. Even though I spent the remainder of the afternoon curled up with my feline roommate catching up on a mystery novel, I can't say Samantha never crossed my mind. Thoughts of her lingered.

During my reporter days, my work didn't stop on the weekend. I remained relentless until I revealed the truth. I wasn't sure if it was the bump on my head from a few years ago or me being over forty, probably both, but I'd learn the art of at least attempting to rest.

For a Monday afternoon, I was surprisingly alert as I watched people mill into First Calvary Baptist Church. Samantha Livingston had a larger turnout for her funeral than I would have imagined. I sat in the back of church and stopped counting at a hundred people. Most of the attendees that sat anxiously on the pews were young. I guessed they were people who went to school with Samantha or may have followed her online.

My first instinct was to flinch when Judith Peters passed by me on her way to the front, but I know she didn't notice me. I was still taken aback by her anger towards me as though it was my fault her soon-to-be ex-husband pursued a young woman. A woman who was practically a member of their family. I wished more than anything that there was another woman captured by my camera lens last Wednesday night. It was apparent Judith would have been hurt, but not quite as devastated.

Speaking of devastation, Judith was practically holding up her daughter, Janine as they trudged down the long middle church aisle. Samantha's best friend was dressed in a slim black dress, with her long black hair pulled back displaying the paleness of her skin. It was the first time I'd seen the girl in person outside of her social media posts. Void of makeup, she still was a beautiful girl. She stared blankly ahead, her eyes red-rimmed. Janine stumbled forward, mainly guided by her mom's grip. Her face reminded me of some tearful moments I had experienced. That point where my brain and facial muscles had grown too exhausted to shed another tear.

My heart went out to her. Grief was overwhelming, especially the closer the loss.

When I lost Aunt C, I was undone. My aunt had been my rock even when her brother, my dad, failed me. When Mama lost it for a while over my dad's rejection and Rev. Lawson's tirades at home were too much, my aunt saved me from my own self-destruction. Her death resulted in the most bitter weeping of my life, even more so than when I walked away from my career.

I wondered how losing her best friend would affect Janine. Did she know the truth about her friend's last night alive? While I didn't care for Judith's anger, deep down I knew the woman wanted to protect her child from Edwin's vulgarity. If I were a mother, I could see never revealing that truth to my own children.

A young man trudged behind the women as though his feet were made of lead. This was my first time seeing Judith's other child too. Ethan Peters was all arms and legs, but at age thirteen he still had a lot more growing to do. I imagined the young man loved Samantha like another older sister too. Probably like any boy, I imagined Ethan admired his dad. That admiration would surely turn to disgust.

After a few minutes of musing about the Peters family, it dawned on me that there were no signs of Edwin Peters. This seemed odd to me. I thought he would have shown his face. Maybe some type of guilt kept him away. *He should be ashamed*, I thought. Edwin may have had an alibi, but the imprint of his hands still remained around Samantha's throat when she died. She probably died with Edwin's DNA still under fingernails.

Maybe Judith ordered Edwin not to attend the funeral. Good for her if she did.

I observed Judith as she sat Janine down in the front row. Ethan slid into the pew next to his mother and sister, his back straight. For some reason, I expected the boy to be more slumped over. Without his dad, the young man seemed to take on the role of being the man of the house. With his dad gone from the house and knowing his parents were heading to a divorce, I couldn't even fathom what was going through his mind.

Out of the corner of my eye, I caught sight of Amir standing next to the funeral director. They spoke in quiet tones. Despite the grief ravishing his face, Amir appeared poised and debonair in his black suit. I saw incredible strength in the man to pull the final arrangements together for his deceased friend. I wanted to talk to him again, hopefully soon after Samantha was placed in her final resting place.

Before I could turn towards the front of the church, I watched Zeke enter along with a few women I recognized from the salon. Zeke was dressed in a black suit, his dreads pulled back to hang down his back. Cherry clung to Zeke's arm, crying bitterly. There were quite a few people crying openly, but Cherry's shoulders shook violently as she tried to walk.

Someone tapped me on my shoulder. I turned to find not only Baldwin, but Moses standing next to the pew where I sat. Both detectives were dressed in black suits, resembling the entourage from the *Men in the Black* movie series. Except, neither were sporting dark shades, and there weren't any aliens in this scene. Though a killer possibly lurked.

I moved down so both detectives could squeeze into the back pew.

Moses eyed me, "I should have known you would be here. Paying your respects?"

I raised an eyebrow, "Same as you."

Baldwin smirked, "We're here to check out the suspects."

I tilted my head, raising an eyebrow as if both detectives had both grown two heads, "Like I said, same as you."

Moses shook his head. "This isn't your case."

"I was one of the last people to see Samantha alive. I'm sorry, fellows, but I feel like I owe it to her to see this through."

Moses glared at me. "We kind of figured that after we heard you went to pay a visit to Edwin last Friday."

I almost yelped, but shut my mouth in time, remembering we were in the back of a church during a funeral. Quietly, I hissed, "If he said something that made him nervous, then he's guilty about something."

Now, both detectives stared at me as if I'd grown some horns.

I huffed, "I wasn't trying to start anything. I was just curious about how this young lady ended up with us attending her funeral today. Alibi or not, something doesn't add up with Edwin."

Moses shushed me as the choir entered the loft and began to sing, *How Great Thou Art.*

I picked up the funeral program to view the hymnal lyrics but stopped on the cover. I'd seen this photo of Samantha on her Instagram profile. She was smiling as if she was letting her little light shine for all to see. It was a sweet, wholesome smile of a young person who had everything going for them.

But that wasn't the case for Samantha at all.

The eulogy by First Calvary Baptist head pastor, Reverend Norman Landon was all of fifteen minutes. One of the differences of attending a predominantly white church, they moved with speed. If this funeral was at any of the black Baptist churches, we'd still be here another hour or more.

I started not to drive in the funeral procession to the gravesite. It had rained most of the weekend, and I knew it would be muddy. But my curiosity won out over my adversity to the mud. Plus, I wanted to go wherever Baldwin and Moses were headed. We were all after the same thing, though I was sure the detectives weren't looking in the directions I was searching.

There was a much smaller crowd at the gravesite. Judith, Janine, Zeke, Cherry and Amir were the familiar faces. I didn't know the others.

Moses and Baldwin hung back, standing near their car. I crept forward and found myself a few feet from Amir. He turned as if he sensed my presence. His eyes were red and swollen, but his grief didn't impact his handsome face. He gave a slight nod to acknowledge me. While Amir didn't seem to mind my presence, one glance over had me face-to-face with Judith. Not only was Judith staring me down, but Janine who surely didn't know me, eyed me with interest too.

I had a sneaky feeling it had something to do with me standing so close to Amir. Janine's eyes cut to Amir and then back to me. As if she suddenly didn't care, she focused on the ground where her best friend would soon be buried.

While Janine's attention turned away from me, Judith kept up her incessant stare which was starting to freak me out. I didn't understand the woman's animosity towards me when all I did was the job assigned to me. After Reverend Landon offered his final words, people began to disperse from the graveside. I didn't want to disturb Amir in his last moments and shifted my feet to walk away.

"Wait."

Amir was still facing the grave, but he'd spoken softly. I couldn't help but wonder if I had imagined him talking.

He wiped at his face and turned. "Thanks for coming. I was hoping to see you again."

I crossed my arms, feeling the wet cold draft through my blazer. "I would love to talk more when it's a better time for you."

Surprisingly, he smiled. "How about this week? Hopefully, I can get the go ahead to clean out Samantha's apartment. I know the landlord wants to get in there and make it ready for the next tenant."

I winced, "Can they just do that?"

He shrugged, "I believe the police did all they could. A crime scene cleaner has been hired, so yeah, I imagine life will go on. I feel bad for the next person to get that apartment."

"Not like Samantha's spirit is going to be hanging around."

His mouth turned up. "No. She hated those kinds of movies. People didn't know this, but she loved the Lord. She gave her life over when she was a little girl. Even when she was shipped around to foster homes, she was always positive. Her grandmother insisted on taking her to church every Sunday. She knew her Bible."

This surprised me for some reason, but when I thought about the photos I'd seen, something radiated from Samantha's face. I also remembered her deep shame last week. Maybe Samantha was shameful of far more than just what people would have thought of her. I knew in my newness I was more conscious than I had ever been in my life of messing up. I knew God gave me a second chance at life again.

Samantha's casket had been completely lowered into the grave. Judith and Janine still sat watching. Judith glanced over at us before turning her attention back to her daughter.

I looked at Amir. "I'm surprised Mr. Peters didn't come. I didn't see him at all today."

Amir didn't turn to look at me, but I could feel anger radiating from his body. "I asked Judith to make sure he didn't come."

I raised an eyebrow, risking a glance at Judith who seemed to be trying to coax Janine up from the chair. "Can I ask why?"

Amir turned to me, "Do you really need to ask? He let her down. He was supposed to be a father figure to here and he turned out to be—"

"May I speak to you?"

Startled, Amir and I both turned to find Judith behind us with her hands clasped in front of her. Since her eyes were directed at me, I assumed she wanted to talk to me.

I faced her, "I'm not sure now is the time."

Judith peered over her shoulder where her daughter still sat staring at the ground where her best friend lay. "No, not now. I want you to come by the house later. Say around six o'clock."

"Okay."

Judith glanced over at Amir. "I hope you can help me with Janine." Her voice broke, "She needs a friend, and I'm not sure how to reach her."

Amir nodded, "Let me help you get her to the car."

Judith bowed her head, "Thank you, Amir."

I watched as Amir placed his arms around Janine, coaxing her to stand up. The girl stood, though she appeared limp. She lifted her face to Amir and wrapped her arms around his neck, clinging to him as though she would fall apart without him. He held her as her cries grew increasingly louder.

The Instagram image of the three friends together flashed in my mind.

Now, there were only two.

I turned and walked away, not wanting to witness anymore grief. Even though I was walking away, my last images of a scared Samantha would not leave me alone. I didn't know if that image would ever go away. If I admitted it to myself, I was angry.

Why couldn't she be saved, Lord? How did the girl escape with her life from one situation only to die a few hours later?

That ultimately kept nipping at the corners of my mind. I'd missed a huge clue somewhere.

After returning to my car, I drove away from the graveside. I needed to prepare to face Judith later. I had no idea why the woman wanted to see me, but my curiosity was piqued. Yes, capturing Samantha on camera with Edwin had to be disturbing, but what was with all the animosity towards me?

I had a feeling I needed to brace myself for more revelations today.

Chapter Sixteen

Monday, 4:08 pm

I decided to kill some time before visiting with Judith. It was also a part of my usual routine to visit with Mama on Mondays. Now, I may seem like a dutiful daughter, but really until last year, I was estranged from Mama. During the years I lived in Charlotte, I came to visit, but I never had that talk on the phone every week kind of relationship with Mama. That was because Mama never quite recovered from my dad walking out on her and leaving her to raise me. Even when she married Reverend Lawson and gave birth to Bev, Mama walked through life shell-shocked.

Dallas Robinson was a handsome, dazzling man, but he never grew up. And he enjoyed his alcohol and chased the ladies up until he died. As far as I knew, despite my rolling stone papa, he never had another child with another woman besides Mama. It appeared, in the beginning, he would settle down. But something spooked him and he ran. I believe Mama was like most women who thought they could fix a man.

I was angry at her for so long, and I felt like, in her misery, she let Reverend Lawson mistreat me because I was my dad's child. Oh, he never laid a hand on me, but his emotional abuse was enough to have me running from Georgetown soon after high school graduation and not looking back for years. I'd overheard Reverend Lawson having a conversation with a church deacon that had run my blood cold against him and everything associated with him, including church.

That no-good Dallas Robinson's daughter.

I was the daughter of the man he hated. The man Mama had never gotten over and everyone knew it. Not that he would ever admit it. That wasn't Christian. I grew to hate Reverend Lawson, a man of perfect standing in the church and community. But his mouth was anything but godly in my book. As an adult, I didn't set foot in the house until he died, and even then, it was only once a year or every other year.

Last year, when Bev responded to one of Mama's episodes, I was forced to see the extent of her mental issues. With Reverend Lawson dead, my mom had become cocooned inside her home surrounded by tons and tons of stuff. The day I entered the house after so many years, I was not only horrified, but devastated by my childhood home. I couldn't believe the amount of crap Mama had accumulated. The memory of entering the crowded home with the small aisles for walking still haunted me. Those memories also stirred up guilt for not understanding the depth of my mother's grief.

Bev and I worked hard with a large cleaning crew to rid the house of hundreds of hoarded items. Whenever I visited, I was always conscience of the small piles of stuff that would appear in the yard or the house. Bev warned me not to scold Mama, but there was no way I wanted to see her succumb to the chaos she'd lived in for so long. That was the least I could do as the eldest child who'd abandoned her for so many years.

I counted it joy when she left the house. On occasion, Mama attended church with Bev and her family, and I'd been able to coax her to my house. Those times out of the house were fraught with anxiety for everyone involved, but worth the effort to see Mama experience air outside those four walls. Since her comfort remained behind the walls of the home where her stuff and her memories lived, we mostly visited her. Like my growing relationship with God, I was grateful to be in Mama's presence now. She did all she could as a woman with a broken heart. Honestly, when it came to matters of the heart, Mama and I were alike. We just handled our broken hearts differently.

She hid, while I ran from one bad situation into worse ones.

Since being back in Georgetown, I'd obtained a key to her house and helped shop for her groceries. Under Mama's watchful eyes, either Bev or I helped her clean the house. The house wasn't immaculate, but it was nowhere near the fire hazard it once was.

Mama had grown accustomed to the routine of seeing me on Mondays, so I didn't want to mess that up. Today, in some strange way, I needed to see her. I needed to get away from the life and death of Samantha Livingston for a while, and I gladly slipped into my own routine.

I unlocked Mama's front door and called out, "Mama, it's Rena."

"I'm back in the kitchen, Rena."

I smiled, thankful that my mom was alert and prepared for my afternoon visit. My smile broadened when I glimpsed her at the kitchen table. She had the bible open with a white mug sitting nearby.

She grinned at me, "I just made a fresh pot of coffee, you want some?"

I pulled out a wooden chair from around the kitchen table that was covered with a floral tablecloth. "Yes, I could use a pick me up right now."

Mama was dressed in a blue tracksuit. Most days she was dressed in a house dress with her robe. It was good to see her dressed in clothes. Her short afro was tinged with more gray, but I could tell she'd tended to it. There was a nice sheen to her hair as if she'd just washed it.

Mama peered at me as she sat the mug down. "You're dressed in black today."

"I just came from a funeral. A young woman I met briefly was killed last week."

Mama frowned, "That's a shame. How old was she?"

"She was twenty."

"That's young. I can barely remember being twenty."

I observed Mama as her eyes glazed over. I was sure thoughts of my dad were probably in her mind. Mama and Dad were on and off from high school until they were both well into their twenties.

She snapped out her memory and smiled at me. The silence between us used to be awkward, but I'd grown accustomed to it. Sipping coffee with your mother was something to be treasured. I knew many people who'd lost their parents and longed for this type of opportunity.

"How are things going at work with Clay?"

"Good. In fact, I met the young woman I was talking about while I was on assignment for Clay."

Mama frowned, "Was she Clay's client?"

"No, but Clay's client knew her."

When I visited with Mama, she always asked about what I did. I found myself sharing with her, not so much the details, but letting her know I did actually have a job. I knew if I shared anything with Mama, she wasn't going to tell anyone.

Then something occurred to me, "Mama, speaking of Clay, do you know Agnes Baker?"

Mama tilted her head as if she was thinking. Then she nodded, "I remember Agnes. We haven't talked in years. She and I used to be friends."

I didn't know this. "Really? She doesn't like me much."

Mama laughed. "She didn't like me after a while either. If she's giving you trouble, it's probably because you look just like your dad."

That surprised me. "Are you saying Agnes had a thing for my dad?"

"Oh yes, Agnes was in love with Dallas. She wanted him to ask her out, but he never did. When Dallas and I started dating, well, let's just say my friendship with Agnes died. She stopped talking to me."

A love triangle. Or kind of... except one of those women, in this case Agnes, didn't get the prize.

Was that really why Agnes was cold towards me?

I reminded her of my dad, a long lost opportunity. That was so long ago though. But from what I knew about Clay's secretary, she'd never married. Most of the time, I was able to keep my dad's escapades in the past where they belonged, but every now and then, Dad's legacy still disturbed me.

For some odd reason, as I sipped more of the coffee, the Instagram image of Samantha with Amir and Janine flashed in my mind. Three friends. Samantha and Amir were close, but how did Janine fit in that photo? At the graveside earlier, Janine had wrapped herself around Amir as he comforted her. I shook my head, not fully understanding why my thoughts had strayed in that direction. Probably because the time for me to leave for the Peters' home was fast approaching.

"How are you and Trey doing?"

I thought I heard Mama's question, but for a few seconds, I wasn't sure I heard her correctly. "Did you just ask about Trey?"

She grinned. "Yes, I was wondering why you two weren't together by now. Bev said you both were close like you were when you were younger."

I cringed. My sister and mom were talking about my love life. That should be normal with most families, I guess, but it just felt plain weird. Neither Bev nor Mama knew how much trouble I'd gotten myself into during my years in Charlotte. I embraced my sexuality during those reckless years despite the after effects of each man I came into contact with. There was no one I could really talk with to discuss how embracing celibacy and battling my feelings towards Trey were a constant struggle.

"Trey and I are friends, Mama. You know he's a minister. One day he may even be a pastor of a church. He probably needs a woman who is..." I lifted my hands and made air quotes, "First Lady material."

Mama frowned. "What kind of person would that be? You forget I was married to a reverend. I'd met Thomas before I met your dad. Even after my wreck of a marriage with Dallas, Thomas was in the wings waiting for me. A broken woman with a child from another man. A man that he didn't like much. I wasn't an ideal first lady."

I frowned. I'd forgotten that Reverend Lawson and Mama were close before she was enraptured with my dad. I inserted, "Still, you attended church every Sunday by Reverend Lawson's side. You were a good woman."

Mama was quiet for a moment. "But I was hurting. Ashamed."

"Ashamed?"

"I don't need to tell you, I never stopped loving Dallas. When your dad asked me to marry him, in the back of my mind, I wondered how long he would commit. I shouldn't have been surprised when he walked away, but it still hurt. Thomas was right there to pick me up. I loved him too. But, I wasn't some perfect first lady. I never even had one of those big hats."

Mama and I both broke out into laughter over that admission.

After we quieted down, Mama's face grew serious. "I know you've been asking God to work on you. We're all a work in progress. I fell apart, and I'm still not sure some days if I will ever be alright, but those days I feel lonely and my sorrows overwhelm, I know God is there." Mama touched the open Bible on her table. "For so many years I went through the motions, but I know when it says God will never leave me, I can trust him."

Mama's brown eyes, which were brighter than I remembered, held mine. "Be careful, Rena. You don't want to let the past overwhelm you and block you from what God has for you. Believe me, I know. Trey is a part of your future, even if you can't see that right now."

I stared at Mama. When I came to visit, I certainly wasn't expecting this. Mama didn't typically dish out advice. Most Mondays, we sat and talked about mundane things. But today, it was like God was prompting Mama to get a message to me.

I swallowed, gripping the mug in front of me. I was trying to absorb this push towards Trey.

Why did I still feel like running?

Chapter Seventeen

Monday, 6:08 pm

I drove to the Peters' family home in a bit of a daze. I was having a hard time shifting my mind from the conversation I had with Mama. I had to admit I felt encouraged. On Saturday, Trey had pretty much said there was no pressure and he wasn't going anywhere. I knew it was time for me to stop running, in theory, but I hadn't quite convinced myself that I could move past the old me. I understood life was brand new now and that God had forgiven me. When was I going to forgive me? That was my issue. When would I feel worthy of the love I struggled to have most of my life?

For now, I had set aside my own personal issues for the business at hand. By the time I turned into the Peters' driveway, I'd braced myself for whatever Judith Peters would throw at me. At least, I told myself I'd be able to handle anything she dished out.

Despite the November weather, the landscape around the two-story home was immaculate. The manicured grass was adorned with orange and yellow mums lining the curves that led up to the stone stairs. I walked slowly, looking from side to side. The front porch covered the front of the house and appeared to wrap around to the other side. The traditional home was stately, reflecting the family's wealth without being over the top.

I rang the doorbell and stepped away from the door. Through the screen door, I could see a wreath made from colorful leaves hanging on the door. I wasn't sure how Judith managed to maintain her impeccable appearance with her husband's discretions. That had to be stressful. Maybe that's why she succumbed to filing for divorce.

The door opened, and Judith appeared looking more haggard than I had ever seen. I wondered if she had been lying down. She raked her fingers through her hair and opened the door wider. "Please come in, Ms. Manchester."

Immediately feeling the warmth, upon stepping inside, I welcomed the heat. The air outside had turned chilly as the sun prepared to set.

Judith closed the door and turned to me. "Thank you for coming by. Follow me back."

I followed as she suggested towards the back part of the house. We entered a large kitchen with stainless steel appliances. The island had a farmhouse sink on one side and gray marble countertops. Sitting conspicuously in the center was a knife block with rows of knives. I didn't like being around objects that could easily be used as weapons, but I also knew it was silly of me to think Judith would do anything to me.

The woman looked like she had aged overnight. Her hair hung limply around her face. She stood behind the island and extended her hand. "You can sit here at the island, I was about to make some coffee. Would you like some?"

"No, I just had a cup at my mother's house. I better not consume any more caffeine today."

"Understood. How about some water?"

I nodded, "Water is good."

Judith opened the double door refrigerator, revealing perfectly lined food containers. She reached down and came back with a bottled water.

I reached for it, "Thank you. You wanted to talk to me about?" I appreciated Judith's hospitality, but I didn't want this to take too long.

The woman tapped her nails on the countertop as if she had to contemplate the best way to talk to me. Finally, she sighed as her shoulders sagged. "I'm sorry."

"Ma'am?" I wasn't sure what to expect, but Judith appeared close to tears.

"I'm sorry for the way I responded to you about all of this. You were doing your job." She swallowed, "Plus, I'm sure if your aunt was alive, she would give me an earful."

Though it was faint, I glimpsed a smile on Judith's face. I had to grin because I could picture my Aunt C giving God an earful about the way Judith had been treating me. This turnabout in Judith's attitude towards me was more than welcome. "My Aunt C would have understood your shock and disappointment over those photos."

Judith nodded. "I know she would have, but not directing my anger towards her niece. Your aunt talked about the hometown girl who grew up to be a big time reporter in Charlotte. She loved you. You were her pride and joy."

I blushed, "I didn't realize Aunt C talked about me to her co-workers."

Judith smiled, "You were the daughter she never had, and you were also the daughter of her beloved brother. So, I apologize and I want to ask you a favor."

"Okay."

"When I saw those photos, they devastated me more than I can admit."

"Because not only did Edwin approach a young woman inappropriately, but her mother was probably of interest to him in the past."

Judith's face paled more than it already was. For a brief moment, she seemed to stand still as if she'd been turned to stone. But she recovered. "You're good. I see you have found out more in the past few days."

"You should know that I met Samantha briefly that night. I followed her home. I wanted to see if she was okay, but I can't get over her fear. I knew she was upset by what happened because she was shaking with fear. Fear for her life kind of shakes."

Judith spread her hands across the marbled countertop as though she needed the structure to hold her up. "The older Samantha became, the more she looked like her mother. Edwin was crazy about Tabitha, Samantha's mom, all during high school. They were high school sweethearts. I don't know what happened, but I suspect Tabitha strayed when Edwin went off to college at Duke. She was not bound for college so she stayed here in town. Got a job at Myrtle Beach for a while, mainly waitressing, I think. She became involved with Samantha's dad. They all knew each other in high school. Tabitha seemed to have more in common with Bruce; they were made for each other. Got married... I was with Edwin by this time, but I could tell he was truly jealous. Tabitha was his first love."

"Edwin described Bruce as a friend. Were they really?"

Judith's eyes widened. "You talked to Edwin?"

"Yes," I placed my elbows on the counter, "I heard Tabitha reached out to him even after she was married, more so after she became a widow."

The paleness was now replaced with a growing reddish tinge around her cheeks. Judith closed her eyes. "Edwin never got over Tabitha. He liked to claim he did, but he didn't."

"Did that make you pause about taking in her child?"

"No," Judith was vehement as though it was a crime for me to suggest otherwise. "I'm a school teacher. I see children in need all the time. My daughter was friends with her, and Samantha was always a joy to be around. She was just dealt the bad luck of losing a dad to war and having a mother who wasn't always there. I had no problem accepting Samantha in our house."

I knew the police asked Judith, but it was my turn. "Where were you last Wednesday evening?"

She narrowed her eyes. "You're not going to do this. I didn't hurt Samantha. I would never hurt another person."

"You still didn't offer where you were."

"The police have my statement. I was here at home. My son can vouch for me."

I held up my hands, "I'm not accusing you of anything. Just checking. Besides, Samantha was killed Wednesday night. You didn't find out about the photos until Thursday morning."

Judith sat still and strangely quiet.

Is she hiding something?

Right before the quiet became unbearable, Judith spoke again. "I called you here for two reasons."

I arched my eyebrow, aware of the abrupt change in subject. "You mentioned you wanted to ask me a favor."

"First, I want you to destroy those photos you took last Wednesday."

I frowned, "I understand they are controversial in the wake of Samantha's death. You want to protect her image?"

"It's more than that." Judith's face crumpled. "My children, especially my daughter, must never know." Her voice fell to a whisper on the last word.

At first, I was stunned. But then I started to understand. Judith didn't want her children to see how low their father could go, and she didn't want to destroy their image of Samantha. "Done. I will make sure all copies are destroyed."

Judith's mouth moved, but she seemed to have lost her voice. I could tell she thanked me, but I never heard the words.

"Was that the only part of the favor? You indicated you had two reasons for asking me over here."

Transforming before my eyes, her back grew straighter. I hadn't noticed the tears leaking down her cheeks until she wiped her face. She sniffled and looked at me, her eyes were set like flint. "You were a good reporter, you know how to dig up information that is not easily found."

I nodded. "I was successful on many occasions for quite a few big stories."

"My husband...soon to-be-ex-husband has some secrets. They're the kind that he protects and hides cautiously. I want you to find out what they are and expose them."

Well, this assignment just changed. "Is this something you discussed with Clay?"

"Not yet, but we can't use what you found last week in my divorce proceedings. I need something harder and a lot stronger."

"You do know what you're asking is way more than you need for a divorce case. Suppose I discover something that sends your husband to criminal court?"

She tossed her head, "Even better. Him behind bars puts him completely out of my children's lives. And now that I think more about this, I want to hire you to do this for me. We can leave your findings out of the divorce proceedings."

I nodded slowly, trying to comprehend this turnabout. "You're asking me to work quietly to find something to take Edwin Peters down?"

"That's correct. Share your fees with me and I will pay you. Whatever you find, it can come out after we're officially divorced."

I was wanting to take Edwin Peters down myself but getting paid to do it... even better. But then, thoughts bombarded my mind. What Judith was doing and my desires to do it, was it the right thing to do? Was this some sort of way to seek revenge?

In the back of my mind, I could hear my brother-in-law's warning to back off from touching whatever gray areas Edwin had dipped in with his business.

I eyed Judith for a few moments, "Can I ask what you expect me to find? Does this have to do with his business dealings?"

Judith raked her fingers through her hair. "That's a place to start. I'm sure you're already aware that I helped Edwin fund Waterway from my inheritance. It's grown beyond that initial one hundred thousand dollars I gave him to establish the business. I imagine millions of dollars go through Waterway from the sales of some of the coastal properties Edwin acquires. I have always had a feeling that Edwin makes a lot more profit than what is listed in his books, but I don't have a way to prove my assumption."

"Does he keep any files here at home that you can access? I'm more than willingly to dig up what I can find, but I have to say, I've not been in the habit of breaking and entering someone's property."

Judith shook her head. "You don't have to do that. I can get you some help, I just need you to guide him where to look based on your hunches."

"He?"

"You've met him already.

"I have?"

"Yes, you were speaking to him at the funeral. Amir."

I don't have hot flashes that I know of, but the kitchen felt really warm all of sudden. "How exactly do you see Amir helping me?"

"He's a computer whiz. He owns a cybersecurity company, and knows how to track down information. He also has access to Edwin's computer system."

"Really?" I felt my eyes stretch wide. "Look, I want to help you, but I need to be assured that going after your husband will not involve illegal measures. I have a license to protect."

Judith answered passionately. "I have just as much claim in my husband's company as he does. I gave him the money to start it. This is about stopping a person's destructive behaviors. Obviously you've seen what Edwin did to poor Samantha. Imagine the effects of his behavior on his own children. It's why I asked you to destroy the evidence you have. Now, I need to go a step further and stop a monster. I need to salvage the company as my children's inheritance."

"You really think Edwin has been doing something criminal?"

Judith scoffed, "I wouldn't put it past him. He's the kind of man who has always liked to cut corners."

"Still, the fallout is going to affect you and your children anyway."

"It will, but not as much if we can get separated from him."

"Thus the divorce and custody of your son, is that your strategy?" I frowned, "You've been with Edwin for twenty-two years. Is there a particular reason why you're filing for divorce now?"

Judith sighed. "I'm just plain tired. I expect to retire from the school district in another five years. It's time I make changes in my life and my children's lives. And..." Her voice trailed off as though she wanted to tell me something else, but something stopped her.

I watched her. Judith seemed to be looking past me. I turned my head to find Janine standing in the doorway. Her eyes looked sleepy, and my first impression was the girl appeared drugged.

Judith moved around the island towards her daughter. "Janine, why are you out of bed? I can bring you what you need."

"I'm fine. I just want some water." Janine shuffled into the kitchen.

I didn't think she noticed me, but after she opened the fridge and grabbed a bottle of water, her attention was on me as soon as she turned around. Her movements seemed sluggish, but her eyes were focused.

"Who are you? Didn't I see you earlier today? You were talking to Amir."

I blinked. The girl's tone was flat. I looked over at Judith, whose look of concern brought me back to my first impression of her daughter at the door.

Was she taking something? The girl was distraught from losing her best friend.

Judith stepped forward. "She's visiting with me. Let me get you back in the bed." She turned to me. "Ms. Manchester, why don't you draw up the paperwork for what we discussed? Hopefully, you can get started soon."

I took her eyes boring into me as my cue to leave. I didn't think Judith and I were finished with our conversation, but I caught the hint. She didn't want Janine knowing why I was there. Judith was going to do whatever she could to protect her children.

"I will be in touch soon, Mrs. Peters," I turned to leave the kitchen. "I'll let myself out."

I sped back down the hall, grateful for another paying gig. Something I'd been wanting for months. How many times in the past few days had I longed to find something on Edwin Peters? And now I had an excuse to do it. Judith's suggestion about Amir's assistance sent waves of excitement through me even more. Not so much the idea of spending time around the handsome young man, a computer whiz was the kind of person I needed on my team.

I would also be able to talk to him more about Samantha. Judith may have wanted me to destroy the photos, but I couldn't forget the ordeal the young woman experienced that day. Undeterred by Edwin's alibi, I still believed Samantha's death could have been the result of his involvement.

I sank down into my car seat, feeling the exhaustion of the day. Despite my weariness and sudden realization that I was starving, a sense of excitement churned in my stomach.

Lord, this is the kind of case I've been asking for. Please help me move forward with caution. Guide me in the direction you want me to go.

As I started the engine, the image of Samantha that played in my head made yet another appearance. While I had acquired a new case, the case I'd taken on without an official client was still a priority.

I added to the prayer.

Please help me find justice for Samantha.

Chapter Eighteen

Tuesday, November 13, 11:16 am

I did what Judith wanted. I destroyed the photos, and something about this task lightened my heavy load. The least I could do was protect the young woman's image. She didn't deserve to have her short life tarnished by Edwin Peters.

I compiled an email and sent it to Clay, telling him about Judith's desire to destroy the photos. I decided to remain quiet about the latter part of Judith's request for now. Knowing Clay expressed misgivings about me checking into Edwin Peters, and that it would get back to my sister, I decided it was best to keep my private gig private. Besides, if what I found and presented to Judith was good enough for her divorce proceedings, Clay would soon have all the ammunition he needed.

I had to admit I wasn't sure about Judith. There seemed to be more she wasn't saying. The woman had so much pent-up animosity about me finding Samantha with Edwin, I couldn't help but wonder if Samantha was alive right now, how Judith would express her resentment towards the girl. *Would she have confronted her?* As a mother, Judith definitely didn't want her children, especially Janine, to find out about the illicit affair. *How would she have gone about reaching out to Samantha or would she have let it go?* It had to be difficult all these years to take on a child from a woman her husband had loved. His first love.

I had to keep telling myself that Samantha was killed the night before, way before Judith found out about the photos.

Suppose she already knew? Women had a sixth sense about their husbands. They noticed oddities. Did Edwin act different around Samantha? Had Judith noticed any signs?

One thing I knew for sure, Judith's assignment last night was clearly about focusing my efforts on bringing Edwin down. Of course, I was more than happy to do just that. The pay was an added bonus.

Clay's office door was closed. Assuming he was with a client, I grabbed a cup of Agnes' coffee. I was prepared to head back to my office when I noticed Agnes watching me. Remembering my conversation with Mama, I decided it was time Agnes and I settle our differences.

"Good morning, Agnes."

She looked at me for a moment. "Good morning." Her brown eyes were luminous and cautious behind her blue-rimmed glasses. "Is the coffee okay?"

I smiled, "Agnes, your coffee is always good. I look forward to having a cup whenever I'm in the office."

A soft smile appeared on her face so briefly that if I wasn't focused on her face, I would have missed the gesture. She returned her attention back to the computer.

While Agnes may have wanted to dismiss me, I wasn't ready to leave the conversation. "I talked to my mom yesterday. Do you know who she is?"

Agnes peered over her glasses at me. "I know your mother. We were friends."

"She mentioned that. You should visit her. It would do her good to reunite with an old friend."

Agnes pursed her lips as if pondering the suggestion. "I heard she wasn't doing too well."

"She's doing better. I think she's in a good place for company."

Agnes nodded. "If you think so. It's been a long time and..." She folded her arms across her chest. "Your mother and I didn't part on good terms."

I wasn't sure what else to say. Somehow I no longer felt it appropriate to bring up my dad. Surely, I didn't think I could connect Agnes with Mama. There was clearly bad history based on jealous emotions from when they were younger, and it was obvious Agnes hadn't gotten over her feelings. When it came to my dad, he'd left a bad taste in my mouth as much as the people he affected. I started back to my office.

I heard Agnes clear her throat behind me. "You look just like him," she stated matter-of-factly.

I spun around, not really believing that Agnes was actually going to bring up my dad.

She stared at me as if observing my facial structure. "You're the pretty version of Dallas. He was such a fun person."

"So I heard." I licked my lips, which felt dry. "We didn't spend a lot of time together, but when we did, he was a fun dad."

"I'm sure if he was here, he'd be proud of you."

Now, I didn't expect this part of the conversation. "That's a nice thing to say, Agnes. I was kind of getting the impression you didn't like me."

She looked sheepish. "I like you just fine. I admire you. You're such a headstrong woman. You say and do exactly what you want to do."

I had to laugh. "I don't know about that, Agnes. I would say the old me used to be that way. The new me knows I can't do anything right by myself. God has shown me a new path, and I'm determined to stay on it."

Agnes grinned. "I've seen you at church. We're all a work in progress. Some days it feels like you're taking two steps forward and ten steps back, but you have to keep the faith. You keep doing what you're doing. I know Clay appreciates your work around here."

Clay's office opened. He looked at the both of us before making a beeline for the coffee. He poured himself a cup and turned to me. "I saw your email. Did you do it already?"

I knew he was referring to destroying the photos. "Yes, this morning."

He nodded. "I guess we'll work on a new game plan."

"Sounds like it." I felt uncomfortable, but I wasn't ready to share his client's request. And I had a right to keep that in confidence. What I did need though was permission from Clay on other matters.

"Clay, I may have an opportunity for another case. Would you be okay if I used my office to make phone calls and meet clients? I understand if you don't want me to, but I don't think I can afford my own office space right now."

He nodded. "Sure. I'm glad you're getting more P.I. work. I'm cognizant that you need to grow your business for the extra income.

"Thank you, bro. I appreciate it."

He winked. "That's what brothers-in-law are for. Just remember to be careful."

I practically skipped back to my office. I scanned the papers Judith had requested on the office copier and emailed the PDF I'd drawn up earlier to her. As soon as I sent the email, my cell phone rang.

I looked down but didn't recognize the phone number.

"Hello."

"Rena?"

The deep voice was familiar. "Yes."

"Hey, it's Amir."

I swiveled around in my chair. "Hey, Amir, how are you?"

"I'm good. I just finished talking to Judith. I was planning to reach out to you later in the week, but Judith seems to think I can help you out with a matter."

I kind of wished Judith wouldn't have sprung this on Amir right now. The man had to be grieving the loss of his friend. "Yes, Judith recommended your services. But really, you need time for yourself right now."

"No, I don't. I could use something to do. If I can help you, believe me, you'll be helping me."

"Okay, well, it's probably best not to get into it on the phone. If you want to swing by my office that would be great. I will be here for a while tonight."

"Sure. Your address is the one on your business card?"

"Yes, that's the correct address."

"Great, I will text you when I'm on my way."

"Sounds like a plan."

I hung up. It was kind of unbelievable that I would be working closely with a guy I'd just met last week. For some reason thoughts of Trey entered my head. We had a sweet time together over the weekend. Somehow, I didn't think Trey would react well to knowing I was working with Amir. He seemed concerned when he saw me talking to Amir last week.

And I felt embarrassed like I'd been caught doing something.

I had a job to do. Hopefully, Trey would understand that. But another part of me thought, *Why does Trey even need to know?*

Chapter Nineteen

Tuesday, 5:20 pm

The first thing I noticed about Amir when he arrived at the office was how young he looked today. During our last two meetings, he'd been dressed in an impeccable suit. Today, he was dressed down in a gray hoodie and blue jeans. He definitely had the Mark Zuckerberg look going, down to his silver wire-framed glasses.

So, he really is a geek. A good-looking geek, but still.

Despite Amir's more laid back, college look, I could smell a woodsy scent about him like maybe he'd just taken a shower. Even with his casual appearance, the man exuded a confidence that accentuated his handsome face. I hated to admit it, but I was kind of smitten with the young man. Handsome and intelligent were characteristics that appealed to me.

I imagined he was really good at what he did, owning a cybersecurity company. In my past, I'd befriended a lot of computer types to tap into materials I needed to report a story. Which made me wonder how far Amir was willing to go. Had he lingered on the dark side of handling sensitive data? The possibility of hacking into Edwin's affairs was definitely inferred by Judith's request.

I reached out to shake his hand. "Thanks for coming."

He firmly held my hand for a few seconds longer before letting go. "Not a problem. Like I said, I wanted to reach out to you anyway." He looked around my office before his eyes landed back on my face. "Working together... this is even better."

His grin was contagious, and a smile spread across my face followed by warmth spreading over my cheeks and down my neck.

Is it bad that I'm looking forward to getting to know this guy and what he can do?

I wasn't sure of Amir's age, but I was pretty sure that I was way too old for him. Probably old enough to be his mother, and that depressing thought wiped the smile from my face. It was time to be serious and tackle the task at hand.

"Have a seat." I waited until he sat in the chair across from my desk. "Would you like anything?"

"No, thanks, I'm fine." He pulled an envelope from his bag and handed it to me.

I reached for it and peeled back the flap. "What's this?"

"That's my standard contract and some information about my company. I realize we've met on at least on two occasions now. I knew you were a private investigator, but you probably just learned about my business."

"Yes, Judith alerted me about your skills last night."
I glanced down at the paperwork and brochure. Both
documents included a very professional Wright
Technologies logo. I loved the logo; it was a simple line
drawing of a lock with a keyhole. I would have to ask
Clay to look over the contract for me. I laid it on my
desk. "I didn't realize you were into computers. When
did all this start for you?"

He smiled deeply showing off his dimples. "I
actually started my business in college. It's how I paid
for my tuition."

I raised an eyebrow. "Oh, I bet you got some good
paying gigs."

"I did, mainly programming for websites and apps."
His smile never wavered, but his eyes were direct as if
expected me to have questions.

I placed my hands on the desk. "You know as a P.I.,
I'm not held down by a lot of logistics like law
enforcement, but I still need to keep my nose clean and
not do anything to jeopardize my license."

He nodded. "I have been known to be creative
around servers and networks, but I can assure you there
will be no problems. I have legitimate access to the
networks that we will be exploring."

Legitimate. I was interested in knowing exactly how
Amir was going to gain access to Waterway's computer
network. Before we jumped into my concerns, there
were other matters I wanted to address first.

I studied Amir's face. I imagined his dressed down
appearance today had to do with his frame of mind.
Despite his smile, his eyes were weary as if he hadn't
been sleeping well. I prodded, "Before we get started,

how are you really doing? Surely, Judith should understand this is a tough time for you and can wait on the information she's requested."

For the first time since he arrived, Amir directed his eyes away from my face. He looked off to the side. I watched his Adam's apple bob as he swallowed. "I'm doing as well as I can after burying a woman who was like a little sister to me. She was the only person I considered family."

"I'm really sorry, Amir. If I were you, someone would have to peel me off the ceiling somewhere."

Amir stared past me, his face downcast. "Last night was the hardest. With everyone gone after the funeral, I really missed her." He licked his lips, straightening his spine in the chair. His eyes focused on me again. "To be honest, if Judith hadn't called me, I would still be wallowing in self-pity right now."

My heart went out to him. I'd only met Samantha briefly, but from the people around her and the outpouring on social media, she had quite the personality. Her pictures seemed to always portray a sweet smile and bright-eyes.

"Judith spoke highly of you. Are you and Janine as close as you were to Samantha?"

Amir stirred in the seat like he wasn't sure how to answer. "I wouldn't say Janine and I are close. Being in foster care together, Sam and I had a different relationship. We had similar circumstances with our moms not being around. She understood me and I her. Don't get me wrong, Janine is fun, but she's …"

"A spoiled, rich girl, perhaps?"

He flashed his dimple. "What makes you say that?"

I shrugged, "I'm assuming. She has wealthy parents. Her mother comes from old money, and her dad is a very successful businessman."

"You're right." He leaned forward, "Janine's cool, but she's definitely high maintenance."

"Would you describe Samantha as high maintenance?"

Eyes wistful, Amir shook his head. "Sam was beautiful inside and out. Not a diva at all. People genuinely loved her."

I leaned forward so I could really look into his face, especially his eyes. "Can I make another assumption?"

Amir raised his eyebrow, his face almost flirtatious. "You're a private investigator, shouldn't you be seeking the facts?"

I smiled back, "Oh, I'm getting to the facts. Let's start with yesterday, you didn't want Edwin Peters to come to Samantha's funeral. Why?"

Amir hadn't disclosed if he knew about Samantha's precarious relationship with Edwin.

"I don't like him. Sometimes, he just looked at Sam all wrong. Like some perv."

I sucked in a breath, uncertain if I should approach the subject. Since I'd destroyed the photos earlier upon Judith's request, I was going to stick to the plan of never revealing what I'd captured on camera last week.

"Sounds like you don't like Edwin Peters. So, Judith explained what she wanted?"

"Yes, and I'll gladly help do whatever needs to be done to take Edwin down. He's not a well-liked guy around here. He gets what he wants by throwing money around, and I'm pretty sure he keeps some high-profile people in his pocket."

I nodded. "We need to look into those people. Still, despite this direction we will be investigating, I wanted you to know that I will continue seeking justice for Samantha too."

There was something on his face I couldn't read. Knowing his grief was still raw, I hung back from saying anything else.

After a brief awkward moment, he said, "Thank you. The police don't seem to be getting anywhere. It's been almost a week since … I found her."

I tilted my head. "Solving cases don't work like they do on television. It takes time to interview people and gather evidence. In essence, it's what I do too."

He nodded, "With your background as a reporter, I have more confidence in you right now. I know you have a history of taking risks."

His comment warmed me, but at the same time, it made me weary. My risks got me into trouble in the past. "So, where should we start with Edwin? How is it that Judith thinks you can get to these sensitive hidden files?"

He smiled, "Easy. I helped install his network at Waterway. I'm able to access information, but I will probably need some help deciphering what I find."

I'm not sure why that surprised me. "Who was responsible for hiring you?"

"Edwin. He was looking to upgrade his system a few years back. He knew the type of work I did and approached me. He wanted a top notch, secure network."

I twirled my pen in my hand, trying to make sure I understood exactly how Amir planned on obtaining this information. "A top notch network where you know all the loopholes and vulnerabilities. This still sounds risky to me. Will he be able to detect you snooping?"

He winked. "I will have to be careful to avoid his IT guy, but I know what I'm doing."

"I see." I was still leery, but with what Judith wanted to obtain, my usual method of tracking down and questioning people could prove fruitless and time-consuming. These days, unless people were extra careful, they left traceable, digital footprints. I imagined that's what Amir would be searching.

Recalling my conversation last Saturday with Trey, I approached my whiteboard. "I was talking to a friend recently about the time he worked at Waterway. This would have been about a decade ago, but he said what prompted him to leave was the rate at which landowners were losing their property. Real estate is all about sales, but I wondered if any property was obtained illegally."

Amir tilted his head. "There all kinds of corrupt stories when it comes to real estate. Sometimes, city officials accept bribes and look the other way when it comes to paying property taxes. I hear contracts can be pretty binding, and once signed, it's a legal battle to renege on deals. I recently read of a case where international players got involved with some high priced condos in Florida. Real estate investments are a great way to hide shady deals. Feds look for offshore bank accounts; but think about the amount of equity that can be in a million dollar home or condo."

As Amir was talking, I wrote topics on the whiteboard.

Taxes. Contracts. Original landowners. International dealing. Investments.

I crossed my arms and reviewed the ideas. "If you can access Edwin's system, I want you to look at some of the larger sales and see if you can find the original owners. If they're still around, maybe we can talk to them. I'm always hearing about the battle between developers and landowners. Is it possible that landowners are not getting their fair share in agreements? Maybe Waterway is pocketing the profits when they resell to developers."

I was talking out loud and circled landowners on the whiteboard.

Amir tapped on his laptop. "Are you looking for owners who maybe didn't want to give up their property?"

I nodded, "Yes, I would like to know what happened to make the deal go through. Were they pressured, tricked, etc.?" The more I stared at the whiteboard, the more I thought it was possible we were on to something. I still didn't know how any of this could relate to Samantha.

I recalled Amir's comment about errands. I turned to look at him. I wasn't sure if this was the right time. "Amir?"

He looked up at me. "Yes."

"I have a sensitive question to ask. I'm not saying any of this ties into Samantha, but you did mention when we met last week that you thought Samantha ran errands for Edwin."

Amir frowned. "That's how she described what she did in exchange for money. I can't say I knew what these errands entailed."

I bit my lip, it was getting late and I was thinking too hard. "She didn't have any kind of diary or any place where she documented her life?"

He shook his head. "Not that I know of. Well, wait..." Amir scrunched his forehead in concentration, "I remember when we were in foster care, she did keep a diary, but she was twelve years old. I don't know if that's a habit she kept. If she did have diary, then the police probably have it now, right?"

"That's a good question. I have some contacts at the Georgetown PD. I can find out."

"You're still trying to tie Samantha's death back to Edwin. Why?"

Without going into details from that night, I considered the best way to explain. "The night Samantha went to see Edwin. She got mad with him and at one point, she slapped him."

Amir's eyes went wide. "She did? What did he do back?"

"Let's say it wasn't pretty."

Amir leaned forward in his chair and swore under his breath. "And the cops don't think he killed her?"

I shrugged. "Edwin has a pretty tight alibi for the period of time that Samantha was killed."

We both sat quietly, only the low whirring of our laptops filled the silence.

Amir looked down at his watch. "Hey, I just realized we missed dinner. Would you like to get something?"

The idea sounded tempting. "I'm actually really tired. I think I'm going to organize my desk and head home. I'm sure my cat is pretty annoyed with me right now."

He beamed, "A cat lady, huh?"

I frowned, "You didn't have to say it like that? I'm not that old."

He'd taken off his glasses. "No, you're hardly old." He focused on my face, his eyes intense. "I looked you up online. You were a reporter for a long time. Do you miss it?"

"I did at one time, but as long I get interesting cases, it feels good being a private investigator. Cases like the one we're working on still require the same tactics to reveal the truth."

"There's quite a few videos of you online. You were... are still gorgeous."

My office seemed a lot warmer than it should be. I didn't realize Amir had been scoping me out that closely. I couldn't talk since I'd checked out all his social media, including several bare-chested photos. "Well, thank you, young man. This old lady appreciates the comments."

He laughed and stood. "You're not that old."

I thought, *No, but I am for you.* He really was a handsome guy. Spending the past few hours with him, I'd managed to tame myself despite my initial reaction to him. He was really easygoing to be around.

Amir reached for his bag. "I'll get back to you in a few days on what I find. Next time, we should eat first. How about I come by during the lunch hour?"

"Sounds like a plan."

We trudged through the dark lobby area of Clay's office. Once Amir stepped outside, I locked the door behind him. I'd enjoyed tossing around ideas with him. After this case, I hoped to work with him more… on a more professional manner, of course.

On my way back to the office, I felt like I was glowing from Amir's comments. Since we're going to be working together, I needed to keep it together.

Besides, if there was a man for me, it would be Trey. Minster Trey Evans. The man I'd known most of my life, not to include, the man who was in my age range. Funny how I'd been running from Trey the past few months and now my hormones wanted to lead me into temptation.

I shook my head. It was late and I needed to feed my stomach.

I often stayed late at the office, but usually I wasn't the last one to leave. Tonight, there was a PTA meeting, and my sister insisted that both Clay and she attend, which was good. I wasn't ready for Clay to know the assignment Judith had for me, so I was grateful I had the office to myself.

After straightening the paper on my desk and shutting down my computer, I'd come back down to earth. I needed to get my head on straight so I could drive home.

Despite it being November, the day had been unusually warm. But the temperature had fallen since sunset, leaving the air crisp but not too cold. I locked the door and headed towards my car.

I paused slightly in my stride towards the car as the hair on the back of my neck prickled. I'd been around a lot shady places and met some of the most interesting people to catch a story, so I'd developed a sense in my gut when something didn't feel right. Right now, as I approached my Honda, I felt someone watching me.

I scanned the parking lot. There were only a few cars, and I couldn't visibly see anyone sitting inside any of the cars.

Amir had just left a few minutes earlier.

Was he still around? Was he watching me?

I'm not sure why my mind locked on Amir. The man had been in my office the last few hours, and other than my old hormones acting up, I didn't get a vibe that I couldn't trust him. He was an intense guy, but the idea of him standing around watching me didn't sit right with me. I was just being paranoid. That was all. But then, maybe that was the problem. Was I too enthralled with the young man's charm to not notice his intentions?

I clicked my key fob to unlock my driver's side door. Once inside, I quickly engaged the locks on the doors, and before starting the engine, I looked around again. I even glanced in my backseat. If this was some *Lifetime* movie, the culprit was always in the back waiting.

Thankfully, the back of my car was clear from any crouching boogieman.

I sighed with relief and started the engine. As I pulled out of the parking lot, a feeling of wanting to laugh crept up in my throat, but it wasn't really a laughing matter.

Something didn't feel right back there.

To add to my paranoia, I circled around and took the long way home. My SIG was in the glove compartment. After cutting the engine, I grabbed it to bring in the house. One of these days, I would carry it on me in a holster, but I hadn't felt the need to do that yet.

Though that might change.

I had a feeling, the more I looked into Edwin Peters, the more moments I would get like this. My brother-in-law had warned me that looking into Edwin's dealings could be dangerous.

Chapter Twenty

Wednesday, November 14, 9:30 pm

I didn't sleep despite my long day on Tuesday. It was officially hump day, and I was feeling sluggish. I checked my email to see if Amir had found anything since we talked last night, but there were no emails. Even if he was a computer whiz, it was silly of me to think he would work that fast.

Since I wasn't the one who could access Waterway's computers, I decided to pursue what I thought I could accomplish. I doubted either Moses or Baldwin would be happy to see me, but the two detectives were on my to do list this morning. A week had passed since Samantha's death. One week since both detectives dropped that bombshell on me. The detectives had to possess more information now. Being overworked, surely they would welcome my help. One could only hope. I stopped by Huddle House and picked up not one, but three cups of coffee. I was regular ole Miss Hospitality today. When I arrived, Deputy Wilson greeted me with his usually warm smile. I handed him a cup of coffee.

"Well, look at my angel, Rena, delivering the goodies this morning."

I winked, "Got to keep you guys caffeinated and awake. Next time, I'll bring donuts."

Deputy Wilson guffawed, "Girl, you too much. What brings you here this morning?"

"Baldwin and Moses here?"

He raised an eyebrow. "Yeah, and neither one of them are probably in a good mood. They were both here until late last night."

I held up the coffee carrier. "I got them covered."

Deputy Wilson shook his head, "You sure like to find trouble, Rena."

More like trouble likes to find me. I grinned and headed back to the detectives' desk.

Both men were hunched over their computers, furiously typing away on their keyboards. I walked up to their desks, but neither one of them noticed me. These guys were definitely out of it and not very alert this morning.

I placed a coffee on Baldwin's desk. He turned his glazed eyes on me. Normally clean shaven, Baldwin was sporting a scruffy gray five o'clock shadow this morning.

"Rough night," I inquired.

Baldwin smiled at me despite the weariness of his body. "Let me guess, you're here to bribe us out of some information." He reached for the cup of coffee and immediately took a sip.

"Bribe. Now that's such a harsh word. I'm just looking out for my two favorite detectives." I turned to Moses who, despite his scowl, accepted the coffee too.

Moses retorted, "Why are you here, Rena?"

I pulled up a chair and placed it in the middle of the two detectives. "I was hoping I could help you."

Moses sighed, "I don't see how. There's not a lot we can share about the investigation."

I nodded, "Okay, well can you share your theory? Like, do you think Samantha let someone in her apartment she knew?"

I'm not sure if it was sleep deprivation or if they wanted to get rid of me by giving me something to work with, but Baldwin blabbed first. "There was no sign of a break-in, so more than likely she knew her killer and let them in the apartment."

Moses added, "Or the killer could have been there when she arrived. We've been throwing around several theories the past few days. What we know for sure is sometime after Samantha arrived home Wednesday night, she lived her final hours facing off with someone she knew who meant to do her harm."

I leaned forward on the chair and thought back to that night. "When Samantha opened the door to me, she closed it slightly behind her. I arrived not too long after she did, saw her walk up the stairs to her apartment. If someone was in there while I was talking to her outside, this person would have had a key to already be in the apartment."

I didn't like where this was going because I knew from my conversation with Amir that he had a key to Samantha's apartment.

I crossed my arms. Samantha's face from that night was still fresh in my mind. "Let's say someone was in her apartment when I showed up, she had an opportunity to get away when I was talking to her. She didn't alert me to any danger. I thought she was just scared about what happened with Edwin, but she could have been scared about who she was facing in the apartment."

Baldwin nodded, "That's the thought path Moses wants to go down. He also wants to pin this on someone too."

"Who?" I asked.

Moses sighed, "Rena, we really don't need to be sharing this information."

Moses or Baldwin didn't need to tell me who they were thinking about. I guessed, but I didn't like it. "I know you questioned Amir since he found her body. He rented the apartment first, and still had a key since they were roommates for a while."

Moses and Baldwin looked at me.

Baldwin asked, "How do you know this?"

"I've talked to Amir on a number of occasions. He's helping me out with a case."

Moses sat up in his chair. "Helping. Helping how?"

I smiled, "Lending me his expertise."

"You know the guy has a record right?" Moses retorted.

I raised my right eyebrow. "What kind of record? Are you saying he's some violent type?"

Baldwin answered, "Not that kind of trouble. Knows his way around computers. Got into trouble when he was younger for hacking into the school district's system. Changed some grades. When he was older, he got bolder about tapping into servers he had no business."

I rolled my eyes, "He was a kid then. Now, he's a respectable businessman, legally running his own company."

"Whatever," Moses exclaimed. "The guy had a key to Samantha's place, and he was the one who found her."

"So, what's his motive?" I said. "Did you find any evidence to connect him? Since he used to live there, his fingerprints would be an issue."

Moses narrowed his eyes, "The neighbors said there were some choice words between Amir and Samantha. They were yelling and cussing at each other loud enough to alarm the neighbors."

I shook my head. "Friends have disagreements. When was this argument?"

Moses narrowed his eyes. "They argued the weekend prior to Samantha's death. So the fact that Mr. Wright has a temper is not something to ignore."

A temper. The man I talked to was pretty mild-mannered. So was Samantha for that matter. I rolled my eyes in disbelief. "So they argued a few days *before* Samantha was killed, what does that have to do with the night she was killed? Sounds like you're grasping at straws. This was a woman who'd been like a little sister to Amir for years. He wouldn't touch her."

Moses leaned forward. "How long have you known this guy? You're awfully defensive about him. He's definitely a person of interest, Rena."

Baldwin interjected, "I'm still wrapping my head around Moses' theory, but people kill those they claim to love all the time. Betrayal or perceived pain can drive someone over the edge."

I'm glad Baldwin wasn't buying into his partner's theory. I didn't believe it. Of course, maybe I just didn't want to see the young man I'd gotten to know as some kind of monster. "I don't see it. He planned his friend's funeral. I spoke to him last night. His grief is genuine. You got to look in another direction. Are you not looking at Edwin Peters at all? The man may have an alibi, but he was the one who attempted to kill Samantha that same night. He should at least have some assault charges."

Baldwin grimaced as he stood to stretch, "Probably, but when Edwin attacked Samantha that was out of our jurisdiction and no charges were filed."

Moses stood from his desk too. "We're doing our jobs. Edwin is completely off the list, but Amir is on the suspect list. If I was you, I would be careful about working with him."

I was almost about to leave when I realized I'd forgotten the most important question. "Hey, I did want to know if you found anything of significance in Samantha's apartment?"

Both detectives stared at me, but it was Moses who broke their silent assessment. "Like what?"

I sighed. "Like a diary, a notebook, something where Samantha could have been keeping track of some activities."

Baldwin narrowed his eyes, "What are you keeping from us, Rena?"

"Nothing. I'm asking you." I slumped my shoulders. Neither one of these detectives had seen the photos which were now destroyed. "Let's just say when Samantha needed money, Edwin Peters was her source.

I heard she ran some errands. Not sure what, but there is a reason why you shouldn't just drop Edwin Peters from your subject list. Those marks around Samantha's neck and I hope some DNA from under her fingers lead back to Edwin. You have my 9-1-1 call to know something went wrong in that house in Pawleys Island."

Moses and Baldwin looked at each other.

Both detectives gave me a head nod, but Moses was the one who answered, "Thanks for the tip. You might actually have been some help today, Ms. Manchester. We'll keep you posted."

"That's good to know. Thank you both for your time." I stood from the seat. I wasn't really pleased about where the detectives were going. Being Miss Hospitality this morning didn't result in any new answers for me.

I didn't like being made uneasy about Amir. What could he have been arguing with Samantha about to cause the neighbors to notice him? I would make it my business to find out. If Amir had something to hide, I couldn't be working with him.

Chapter Twenty-One

Thursday, November 15, 1:40 pm

Being a private investigator was not a glamorous career. Actually, neither was being a reporter back in the day. There was a tremendous amount of grunt work to find clues to the truth. My problem was I still had no clue what to look for on Edwin Peters. Amir delivered on the data which I was tediously opening, one file after another. I started with Waterway's financial records, not really comprehending what I was viewing. Staking out Edwin in my car like I'd done last week seemed more exciting than this. Probably because I was searching for something to magically appear before my eyes.

When Amir arrived on Thursday, he kept his promise and brought food. It was early afternoon, but I'd skipped lunch. The smell of fresh egg rolls and chicken lo mein wafted into my office. The sight of him perked me out of the funk I'd fallen into while slugging through data. Despite Moses' suspicions of Amir, I still had a case to work and bills that needed to get paid regardless. Since the young man brought food, he was a saint in my book.

"You have no idea how happy you've made me with those greasy, brown bags."

Amir was dressed casual again today. I'd come to the conclusion that jeans and a hoodie was his normal dress code. The days I saw him in a suit was for that particular occasion, one being a meeting and the other a funeral. He grinned, "I knew you were hard at work. You probably forgot to eat lunch."

I raised my eyebrow. "How did you know I skipped lunch?"

He winked, "Just a hunch. You are one focused woman. I imagine you stick with cases until you can solve them or get to the truth."

I smirked. "I am a bit tenacious... to a fault."

"I'm the same way, I could get lost in code for hours."

We sat and munched on food for about ten minutes. I felt comfortable with the silence between us. It wasn't bad, but I could have just been really hungry too. I gobbled down the lo mein noodles.

Amir sat his carton of almost eaten lo mein down on the table and looked over at me. "I think I found something."

I raised my eyebrow. "Really?"

"Yeah, did you know Edwin Peters owns quite a few properties?"

I frowned, "Under Waterway?"

"Actually, not Waterway. That's what drew my attention."

I sat up in the chair. "Not Waterway? Some other company, then?"

"Yes. Here, look." Amir pulled out his laptop and slid his chair next to mine.

With his closeness, I could smell the same woodsy scent that had become familiar every time I was near Amir.

He pointed to the screen. "When I did a search, I found two properties, one in Georgetown and the other in Horry County, owned and operated by Oceanic Real Estate. Digging further into Oceanic, I discovered it's associated with Ethan Peters."

I frowned, "Erin? Edwin's thirteen year-old son? He bought property in his son's name. Can he do that?"

"I don't know if it's legit, but that's the way it appears on the LLC paperwork. The address associated with the LLC is the same address Waterway used about ten years ago."

I grimaced, "So this company was set up about ten years ago using the address that used to be Waterway? His son would have been like three years old back then." I pondered that for a minute, "Did Edwin move into a new building, thus the change of address?"

Amir nodded, "Yes, Edwin moved the official headquarters of Waterway to the building where it is now, but he has several other branches of Waterway."

"Okay. Is there anything else suspicious about Oceanic, other than the property being registered to a toddler, now teenager? Did Edwin set this up for his son to inherit later or something like that?"

"That's the way it could appear. Both of these properties are worth a lot of money. We're talking millions if they were sold to the right developer.

According to this map, the properties are in prime locations."

I sat back in my seat, my almost eaten carton of chicken lo mein now forgotten about. I closed the carton lid and grabbed the rest of my egg roll. As I munched, I tried to ponder how important Amir's find was and what could we do with it.

I didn't want to bring it up, but I felt the need to warn Amir about my conversation yesterday. "Have you heard from the detectives on Samantha's case?"

He squared his shoulders and turned to me, eyes wide at my sudden change of subject. "No, I haven't heard from them. Why? Have you heard something?"

I bit my lip, knowing Moses and Baldwin wouldn't be pleased that I was talking to Amir. "How long did they question you after you found Samantha?"

He shrugged. "Hours, but they let me go since I had an alibi."

"Which was?"

He narrowed his eyes. "I was working late that night. I have clients who can back up my story. I helped them setup a security system in their office. I didn't get home until almost midnight. She called me earlier, right before I grabbed some dinner. I could tell something was wrong, but she said she was okay. After I left my client's house, I thought about checking on her, but I was too tired. I don't know, maybe I should have drove by. If I'd gotten their sooner..."

I reached over and patted his hand. "There's nothing you could have done, Amir. Her death was immediate."

He sucked in a breath, blinking back tears.

"I told you I wanted to make some headway on Samantha's death too."

He wiped his face. "You did. Are you still trying to connect her death to Edwin?"

"I'm following the evidence as it is revealed to me." I sighed, "Amir, who else would have visited Samantha that late at night? We need some suspects."

Amir smirked. "Well, just as long as I'm not on the list."

"Just know that the police are trying to narrow down the suspects, and you're not completely off their radar since you have a key to Samantha's place."

Amir rubbed his hands across his face. "That's just great."

"Also, one of Samantha's neighbors complained about hearing you arguing with Samantha, very loudly, with some choice words the prior weekend."

"What? Oh, come on." Amir closed his eyes. He was quiet for what felt like a full sixty seconds. Finally, he spoke, "We rarely argued, but when we did, it was always fierce. She would say, 'You're not my real brother.' That's what she said that night. I knew she was late on the rent again. I saw the notice by the door. It was a big yellow Rent Due card, so I fussed at her. She said she would get the money."

Amir got up from the chair. "I told her to let me pay it. She said she already had the money and would have everything caught up by the end of the week."

He crossed his arms. "So typical of her. When she said, 'You're not my real brother,' I lost it. I asked her, 'Is Edwin your real dad?' That's what I said to her, and she started yelling and cussing. Next thing I know, she was crying and telling me to get out. So I did."

His voice cracked. "I called her Monday night. She didn't pick up the phone. I called her Tuesday. She reached out to me Wednesday night and told me she was okay. She didn't sound right. I should have gone to see her."

I stood and walked over to him. "Don't do this to yourself. Believe me, I was there. If someone was there that night, I didn't know." I guided him back to where we were sitting.

He sat down, his eyes now red with emotion. "I've been in shock this past week, but now I'm just angry. Who did this?"

I moved my chair next to him and countered his question, "Who else could have visited Samantha that night? Who else has a key to her place?"

Amir crossed his arms, "I don't know if the cops know this, but Samantha's friend stayed with her for about a month."

"Who?"

"She worked at the salon with Samantha. I've only met her a few times. She was at the funeral on Monday. I think she's the owner's niece."

I tried to recall who was at the funeral, "Cherry?"

Amir snapped his fingers. "That's it."

"I met her at the salon. She was really broke up about Samantha's death."

"Yeah, well, from what I recall Cherry had a rough time with her boyfriend. I think Sam said he might have hit her. Cherry showed up one night scared with bruises all over her face and arms. Sam did what any good friend would do, she opened her door for Cherry to stay."

"So Cherry's boyfriend was abusive? He could have been upset about Cherry leaving him to stay with Samantha. Do you know anything about the guy?"

Amir shook his head. "No, I don't."

I blew out a breath. I needed to visit with Cherry. It's possible Samantha could have given her a key. "You said Cherry only stayed a month?"

"Yeah, I believe Samantha mentioned she moved back in with her aunt."

"Then that doesn't make sense about Cherry's boyfriend…"

There was knock at my office door. I looked at my watch seeing that it was almost three o'clock. "Come in," I called out.

When the office door opened, I expected to see Clay or Agnes. Instead, Trey walked through the door. By the stunned expression on his face, I'm sure seeing Amir in my office along with the Chinese food containers wasn't a pleasant sight. And, I hadn't noticed until the door opened how close I was sitting to Amir. We were side by side like we were having the most intimate conversation.

Chapter Twenty-Two

Thursday, November 15, 3:08 pm

I could've sworn I saw a brief flash of anger in Trey's eyes, and he wasn't one to anger easily. Trey was one of the most good-natured men I knew. I pushed my chair a little away from Amir before standing, not sure why I was feeling so guilty. We were just talking. In fact, the conversation before Trey stepped through the door was just getting to some information I wasn't privy to and really needed to know.

Trey looked at me, "Sorry, I didn't mean to disturb you. You weren't answering your cell phone."

I answered, "Oh." What else could I say? I peered down at my phone which I had silenced and saw several messages. Some from Trey and a few from my sister. "Is everything okay? I see a message from Bev."

Trey stepped further into the room as if he was being cautious, staking out what really had been going on behind closed doors. He answered with tightness in his voice, "Yes, she was trying to get in touch with Clay. I just saw Agnes who said Clay was in court. Bev thought you could help if you weren't too busy."

It could have been my imagination, but Trey drew out the words, "too busy" a bit sarcastically. I watched Trey glance over at Amir.

Amir had closed up his laptop and was packing it into his bag. He wasn't looking at either one of us. I think he sensed it was time to end our meeting.

"What's going on?" I asked.

Trey's eyes were still on Amir. "Brittany got sick at school, and she was hoping to get you to watch her."

"Oh, I can do that. I will reach out to Bev."

Feeling the awkwardness creep into the room with the two men, Trey staring Amir down while Amir casually cleaned up the cartons of Chinese food on my desk, I sighed, "I guess it's time you two officially met each other. Trey, this is Amir Wright. He's the owner of Wright Technologies. We're teaming up on a case."

I turned towards Amir who was now outwardly sizing up Trey.

"Amir, this is Minister Trey Evans. My long-time friend. We've known each other since we were kids."

Amir placed his bag on his shoulder and looked over at Trey. He smiled, but it wasn't the full wattage version he always gave me. "Nice to meet you, Minister Evans." He reached his hand out towards Trey.

Trey hesitated for a second before returning the handshake. "Likewise."

I didn't realize I'd been holding my breath until I felt the release of air from my lungs.

Amir turned to me. "I will continue to dig into the data I find. Let me know if you want me to make any further connections with what I found so far or if you want me to go in another direction."

"Thanks, Amir, I will."

"Enjoy your afternoon." With that, Amir left my office leaving me standing with Trey.

"I should probably call Bev to see if she still needs me to watch Brittany." I reached for my phone, but then stopped. I cocked my head to the side and looked up at Trey. "So, why did my sister reach out to you?"

Trey shrugged. "I have no idea. I guess she figured I could get in touch with you. Seems you were a bit too preoccupied for either of us today."

I narrowed my eyes. "I'm sorry, I had my phone silenced. I am getting paid by a client and time is a factor. Even though I work for myself, my hours aren't that flexible."

"Of course." Trey answered curtly.

I wasn't really feeling the vibe I was getting from him. I knew he wasn't pleased to see Amir. This was the second time I'd been around another man, something Trey hadn't seen since I'd been back home. I was sure it was disconcerting to him, especially with the way I'd been avoiding him lately.

"You want to have a seat, let me call Bev and then we can talk."

Trey look like he wanted to bolt, but he walked over to the chair where Amir had just been sitting. He sat on the edge of the seat as if he was posing to leave in a hurry.

I dialed Bev. "Hey, Sis. Sorry I missed your calls. Is Brittany okay?"

"Hey, no problem. She's laying down now. I figured you and Clay were tied up. I was in a session with one of my more troubled kids and just didn't know what to do."

Bev was a guidance counselor, and her "other" kids were extremely important to her.

"It sounds like things worked out."

She sighed, "It did, I made an appointment for tomorrow. The young lady really needs help, especially now that she's been placed in her second foster care home."

"Oh my, that is troubling. I can stop by on my way home tonight and visit. Let me know if you need me to pick up anything."

"Thanks, Sis. I appreciate you checking in. I know you're busy. Clay told me you have new clients, that's wonderful. You will have to tell me about them soon."

I grimaced. My baby sister didn't need to know about this client or the assignment, I already knew she wouldn't approve. I ended the call and turned my attention to Trey.

He had gotten up from the chair and was standing by the whiteboard.

"I'm sorry, Trey. I will do better about not being so focused on a case."

He turned to observe me. "What kind of case are you working on, Rena? Are you looking into Edwin Peters?"

I glanced at the whiteboard noticing I had Waterway underlined at the top. I probably should have erased that. "Yes, but I can't get into the details."

He frowned, "And this Amir guy, how is he helping you?"

"He's helping me access data and …" I held up my hand. "That's all you need to know, Trey."

He frowned, "You need to be careful, Rena. Edwin Peters is a pretty powerful guy around here. You don't need to be getting yourself into any trouble."

I sighed. "I can handle myself, Trey. My career for years was built on exposing the truth."

He looked back at the board and the topics I listed. "Why is landowners circled?"

"It's an area of interest that I'm looking at, Trey."

He stepped away from the board. "I don't have a good feeling about this, Rena."

Suddenly a wave of anger rushed over me. I wanted to know why I was feeling guilty about doing my job. Sure, Amir was an attractive guy, that certainly got my attention, but we were working on a case for a legitimate client. I was not happy about Trey interrogating me. "Are you sure your feelings are about my work or the fact that I'm working with Amir?"

He smirked, "You said you just met him."

He is definitely annoyed about Amir. Go figure!

"I did just meet him last week. He came highly recommended by my client. We're making good headway on the case. It's all good. You have nothing to worry about."

"You're awfully chummy with a guy you have only known for a week."

"We're working on a case together. Plus, he was close to Samantha Livingston. We were talking about suspects."

"You were talking about a murder case?"

"Yes, Trey. I talked to Moses and Baldwin yesterday about the same case."

"So, you're involved in a murder case and investigating Edwin Peters?"

"Yes. What is wrong with that? It's what I do."

He lifted his hands, "I don't know. I guess it just bothers me."

I narrowed my eyes. "That I'm working on cases I'm passionate about solving? Or are you just jealous?"

He looked at me incredulously, "What?"

"Admit it. It bothers you to see me with another guy, no matter the fact that we're working on a case professionally."

"That's not it." Trey's words faded as he protested.

"Then what?"

Trey looked away, his silence speaking volumes to me.

"I'm sorry this bothers you." I added before I could stop myself. "Do you know why it seems like I avoid you?"

He swung back to face me.

I plowed ahead, "You have always had this higher level thinking about you, even when we were younger. You were a star athlete and people loved you. People always looked down on me because of who my dad was."

He shook his head, "That's not true. What does that have to do with anything?"

"Plenty!" I shouted. "You know who you reminded me of just now? I will tell you. Reverend Lawson."

Trey flinched.

"Oh yeah, he was held in the highest regard. Ultimate respect, but he tore me down every chance he got. You are held in the highest regard. And right now, I feel like you just waltzed in here and looked down on what I do, like this shouldn't be what I'm supposed to be doing. That I shouldn't care about a young woman who was murdered or the fact that a powerful man is responsible in some way. When I see injustice, I don't sleep at night, Trey. I have always fought to find the truth. I did it my entire career."

My face grew warm, and I knew tears were not far away. "There are so many things about me that I'm ashamed of because my goal in the past was to always expose the truth no matter what it took. I feel unworthy to be around you sometimes. If you only knew how damaged I was..."

"Rena..." Trey pleaded.

I ignored him. "You said last Saturday we were friends. No pressure. You would be here for me. I'm trying to get back to the person I was, but be a better person than that ambitious, story chasing reporter I once was. I still did a lot of good when I was a reporter. I miss that. It's why I took up being a private investigator. The stuff that I do... I will do my best to not ever cross lines like I would have in the past, but I want to do this and I need people to stop questioning what I'm doing."

Trey grabbed my shoulders. "I'm not questioning you. I'm just worried. I meant what I told you."

As I examined his face, I could definitely see worry in his eyes. It could have been my emotions, but I also sensed Trey might be thinking I was imbalanced.

He let go of my shoulders slowly as if he thought I would topple over when he let me go. I didn't.

But I felt really stupid. That's what I called a conversation going sideways.

Why did I just blurt all that out?

If Trey didn't understand I was damaged goods, he had a pretty good idea now.

Chapter Twenty-Three

Monday, November 19, 12:40 pm

I stayed hidden in my cave for most of the weekend. I didn't venture outside my house nor did I answer the phone. Trey called twice on Saturday, but I ignored his calls. I wasn't even mad with him. I was angry with myself because I'd come off like the insecure girl I once was, and I'd always thought of myself as having grown past that damaged girl. I was, after all, a grown woman.

Sunday, Trey texted: **I'm here for you**.

I wrote back: **I know.** That made me cry. I truly didn't understand my outburst at Trey. He was only showing me he was worried. It was wrong to compare him to Reverend Lawson. Trey had never treated me like my stepfather did, and he had always been in my corner when we were younger. And for all appearances, Trey had a right to be worried seeing me around a strange man. I knew the content on the whiteboard in my office didn't help my case.

I felt guilty about the one person's phone call I did answer, and the irony fell on me so hard. Amir called.

"I talked to Cherry and she definitely had a key, but the interesting thing is she said she lost it."

I'd been lying in bed glued to my laptop, but this new information caused me to sit up. "Really, when?"

"Cherry said about a week before she moved out. She actually lost her purse and had to cancel all her cards."

I gasped. "Her purse was stolen?"

"Sounds like it. Still, with her purse being stolen, it would have had to be someone who knew Cherry had been staying with her and had a key. I have to say, someone targeting Samantha for that length of time really bothers me."

I wasn't feeling the theory either, but someone had found a way to access Samantha's apartment. "Do you know if Samantha had any issues online with social media? She had a lot of followers on Instagram. How careful do you think she was with her personal information?"

Amir sighed, "I think she was pretty careful, although I know she got some nasty comments and messages. I'll look back at her feeds, but I don't see one of her followers tracking her down either."

"Yea, I guess that is pretty far-fetched. I'm going to swing by and visit Cherry later today. I've been wanting to talk to her aunt who happened to be friends with Samantha's mom."

"Really?" Amir exclaimed. "Now that's a connection I didn't know about. Let me know what you find out."

"Will do."

Two hours later, I drove out to Andrews, a small community in Georgetown. I had reached out to Zeke's sister using the phone number he gave me a few weekends ago. Yvette responded and was willing to answer my questions. I didn't realize at the time that Cherry was Zeke and Yvette's niece. The young woman had moved in with her aunt only a few weeks ago. It occurred to me if Cherry had still been staying with Samantha, her friend might be alive. Or, there could have been two young women dead. I wondered if this was something that bothered Cherry.

When I arrived at the doublewide trailer, Cherry walked out onto a porch that seemed to be held up by stone blocks. She stood, waiting for me to exit my car.

"Hello, Cherry. It's good to see you."

"Hello, Ms. Manchester. Come inside. My aunt is waiting for you."

I stepped inside the trailer, greeted by a steamy warmth compared to the temperature outside. I glanced around and saw an older woman behind a kitchen counter, chopping up something. She glanced up. Her ebony skin was shiny with sweat. She reached for a towel to wipe her face. Yvette was definitely Zeke's sister. She was just as tall as her brother, but her weight was massive with most of it being around her hips. She swayed as she walked almost like she was waddling. "Hello, Ms. Manchester. My brother Zeke mentioned how pretty you were."

My face warmed even more. I held out my hand. "Thank you for seeing me."

Yvette wiped her forehead again and then rubbed her hands before she shook mine. I noticed her hand had a slight tremor when I shook it.

"I hope I can help you. We're all broke up about Sam. She was the sweetest thing. Her offering her place to Cherry was a really nice gesture. That old boyfriend of Cherry's was here at my house looking for her every night for a while."

I turned to Cherry, "Oh, I hope he's not a problem still."

Cherry waved her hand, "Nope, he's in jail now."

"For a long time, we pray," Yvette responded. "What can I do for you?"

"Zeke mentioned you were friends with Samantha's mother."

Yvette sat down heavily in a chair. "Won't you have a seat?"

I smiled, taking a seat on the sofa.

Cherry went to lean on the armrest of the chair where her aunt sat, her eyes riveted on me.

After everyone seemed settled, Yvette finally responded. "Tabitha and I were good friends from grade school until we graduated. Well, I should say at least until our senior year. That's when Edwin went away to school, and Tabitha started hanging out with the wrong crowd."

"Really? They were dating?"

"Yeah, Tabitha had a lot going for her. Believe it or not, back then, we both were cheerleaders." Yvette's belly jiggled as she laughed. "Edwin was the star running back... Hmph, all that seems like ancient history now."

Yvette seemed to sober at the memories of her past. "Tabitha didn't live that far from here. Her family lived in the trailer park down the road. I want to say Tabitha's brother still lives there."

I leaned forward, "So Sam still had family after her grandmother died?"

Yvette nodded, "Yes, but Sam's uncle wasn't suited for raising a little girl. He's a known alcoholic. Probably doesn't have much of a liver left by now. Anyway, when her grandmother got sick and could no longer care for Sam, the Peters convinced the family judge to let them raise her."

I leaned forward. "Can you tell me more about Tabitha?"

Yvette nodded, "Tabitha started drinking during our senior year. She kind of was lost after graduation, but she got a job, a car and a place at the beach. There were some rumors about her job."

"What kind of rumors," I asked.

Yvette sighed. "A couple of fellows said they saw Tabitha dancing in one of those strip joints."

"Oh," I let out a breath.

"Yeah, I was kind of shocked. Tabitha was the best cheerleader, team captain. That girl could do all kinds of flips, but she was also one of those girls who was a little too flirty. Anyway, Bruce must have heard and he helped her get another job, waitressing or something. I guess she was okay with it, she started dating Bruce." Yvette looked like she'd gone back in the past. She finally spoke again. "Bruce was good for her. He treated her right."

I nodded. "I heard Bruce and Edwin were friends."

Yvette peered at me. "They were good friends. Bruce was the quarterback. He got more accolades then Edwin did, but they still seemed to be good-natured."

"Bruce went into the military?"

"Yeah, after Samantha was born. He wanted to do more, and the military offered him a chance to stretch his wings and earn more money for his family. All he'd been doing was working as a mechanic in his dad's shop. If he had the grades, he probably could have gotten a scholarship, but Bruce wasn't much of a book person."

I inquired, "Edwin was?"

Yvette chuckled. "Believe it or not, Edwin was a smart cookie. He was wheeling and dealing, even back then."

Her comment piqued my curiosity. "What do you mean by that?"

"Well, Edwin's old man was a hustler, and he raised his son to be the same. Mr. Rochester Peters owned a lot of land and houses. Some of it he gambled away, but he always earned his money back. I'd heard the old man even won some land in a bet."

Interesting. I wondered how much of an influence Edwin's dad had on him. Did the older Peters patriarch delve into illegal matters too? "So, Edwin's dad was into real estate too? I heard Mrs. Peters helped Edwin establish his business."

Yvette nodded. "That's about right. Remember, I said his dad like to gamble. When he died, he didn't have much to leave his family. Judith was in the class ahead of us, so I didn't know much about her, but I knew her family was wealthy."

"I've been told Samantha went to Edwin whenever she was in a financial bind. Is this true?"

Yvette nodded. "She did like her Mama. Edwin practically supported Tabitha right before she overdosed, and when I say support, he gave her money that went straight to her heroin addiction. I don't think Edwin understood this until later. He thought he was helping out his high school sweetheart." Yvette shifted her weight in the chair. "To answer your question, I'm sure Samantha knew Edwin was a source for her mama. That family took her in, so it became natural for her to ask."

Until this point, I hadn't been looking at Cherry. I observed her peeling something off her nails, probably the black nail polish she was wearing. "Cherry, during the time you lived with Samantha, did you notice when she went to Edwin?"

Cherry shook her head. "No, I didn't. I helped out with the rent for the short time I stayed though. I don't think she needed help until after I left."

"When did you move out?" I asked.

Cherry stiffened, "It was the week before she…"

I continued for her, "She passed away. Your boyfriend was here harassing your aunt, he never found out you moved in with Samantha?"

Cherry looked alarmed by my question. Finally, she responded, "No, he couldn't have done anything to her. I moved back with my aunt once he was in jail."

"Oh, I see."

Cherry swiped the tears fully flowing down her face. "It was nice to have a roommate. Samantha was sweet and a lot of fun. I'm really missing her. When my aunt needed to have her surgery, I felt it was best to move back here."

Yvette peered at her niece. "If I hadn't had my surgery, would you have stayed with Samantha?"

Cherry's eyes flooded with more tears. "Maybe. I kind of wish I was there that night. If I was, maybe nobody would have bothered her."

Her aunt answered sharply, "Or you could be dead."

I didn't want the aunt and niece at odds with each other, but I agreed with her aunt. "Cherry, you told Amir you lost your purse with Samantha's key. Where did you lose it?"

Cherry twisted her hands. "I went to this club down at the beach that Samantha had been raving about. I went to dance and when I came back, my purse was gone. Somebody was supposed to watch it, but I guess everyone went to the dance floor too. It was stupid of me to bring it inside. I should have left it in the trunk of the car."

I asked, "Which weekend was this?"

"I moved my stuff out that Friday. I drove back up to ride with Samantha to the beach for the weekend."

Cherry lost the key the weekend before Samantha was killed. This didn't seemed like a coincidence to me.

"Who knew you were staying with Samantha?"

Cherry wrinkled her nose in concentration. "My aunt and Uncle Zeke. I'm guessing Samantha told Amir. She told him everything."

I agreed. "That's make sense. They were like brother and sister."

Cherry had a silly grin on her face. "Sort of."

I raised my eyebrow at Cherry. "They were more than friends?"

Cherry shook her head. "No, no. I think Samantha had a crush on Amir, but because he thought of her as a younger sister, she didn't try to pursue anything. That would have been too embarrassing."

Somehow I could relate to this. When I was younger, I crushed on Trey who thought of me like a sister—least he did back then.

My mind recalled photos I'd seen in the past week. "Cherry, when I was at the salon, you mentioned Janine Peters wasn't really a friend. What did you mean by that?"

Cherry took in a deep breath. "I could be reading too much into her, but Janine was jealous of Samantha. At least it seemed that way to me."

I tilted my head, interested in where this was going. "How so? Looking at the two women, Janine had more."

Cherry twisted her mouth, "Yeah, materially, but she has no personality. Janine comes off as one of those stuck-up, mean girls. She sounds like she's trying to be funny or sarcastic, but she's really being mean. Sam could never see this. When I mentioned it, Sam said, 'That's just Janine.'"

"Sounds like Samantha was really accepting."

Cherry tossed her head like she couldn't believe this herself. "Yeah. Too accepting. But it was obvious to anyone Samantha was prettier, had more followers, got more attention and was definitely sweeter to be around. Janine thinks she's better than everyone else and doesn't seem to understand that just because her parents are rich doesn't mean people will automatically like her."

Cherry was quiet for a while, but I could tell she had more to say. The one person I hadn't focused on was

Janine Peters. Assuming the girls were best friends and how grief-stricken the girl was, I'd let her slip my mind. The girl's father was who I was after.

Cherry twisted her fingers as if she was nervous. "One night, when we were up talking, I asked her why she let Janine treat her the way she did. Sam said she felt bad for Janine. That just because people had money didn't mean they had it all together. I still felt like she should've dropped her as a friend. Even Amir thought that too."

That surprised me. "He did?"

"Yeah, Janine was always hanging on Amir. He's way older than her, and he just wasn't into her. I think he's like twenty-six, and Janine can act really immature. Anyway, he put up with her because she was Sam's friend."

Yvette had been quiet as I spoke to Cherry. She spoke up, "Sounds like the Peters weren't good for Sam. They seemed to have more of a negative impact on her even though they helped her get out of foster care."

I couldn't agree more with Yvette.

Now, I was starting to see why Judith didn't want Janine to ever find those photos of her best friend. I imagined that would have been an explosive situation.

Chapter Twenty-Four

Thanksgiving Day.

Thursday, November 22, 12:07 pm

It was Thanksgiving and probably the first real holiday I decided to take off all year. I stopped by Mama's house to pick her up. Mama hadn't been out the house in a few weeks. When I arrived, she was already dressed in another tracksuit. This one was burgundy. I wasn't sure if Mama was shopping online again or if Bev had been buying these suits for her. Despite her casual, youthful appearance, Mama had a nervous smile on her face.

Beside her were some bags.

"What's in the bag?"

Mama smiled, "I made two sweet potato pies and an upside down cake."

I grinned, "Well, you've been busy. How come you didn't pass any cooking skills down to me? Bev is quite the cook."

Mama winked, "You still have time to learn."

Not. I would leave the cooking to everyone else. Eating was good enough for me.

I was glad Mama had spent some time helping Bev with the food. Bev had mentioned she'd invited quite a few people over for Thanksgiving this year, and I was a bit worried about Mama. Mama was used to being around family, but she tended to withdraw with more people around her.

The ride over to Bev's house was quiet. I was still processing the last week. I thought about the cases, but for some reason, I mainly kept thinking about Trey. After my response to his text on Sunday, he hadn't reached out anymore. I wasn't sure if he thought it best for me to reach out on my own. I mean the last time he pushed, I kind of tipped over the edge. But hey, transparency was good for the relationship. Or, was it not? I still had lingering feelings that I'd said too much.

Yesterday, Bev told me she'd invited Trey and Joseph over for Thanksgiving. I'm sure seeing him today wasn't helping my anxiety either.

This morning, before I left to pick up Mama, I decided to text **Happy Thanksgiving** to Amir. I knew he was going to be spending the holidays alone, and with just losing Samantha, his oldest friend, that had to be hard. I kind of wanted to invite him over for Thanksgiving but settled on that not being a good idea.

He texted back that he had some promising data and asked if we could get together later today or Friday. I decided I to wrap up some leftovers for him and see him after I dropped Mama back home. Amir was a really attractive guy, but there was at least a sixteen year age gap between us. After finding out his age from Cherry, I had firmly settled on being a big sister.

I helped Mama carry in her bags when we arrived at Bev's house.

Despite being the main cook for the day, Bev squealed like a little girl when she pulled Mama's pies out of the bag. "Mama, thank you. I appreciate you baking all of this."

Mama smiled, "It was the least I could do. Where are my grandbabies?"

"Brittany and Tiffany are watching television in the family room."

"Good, I'm going to sit with them."

I watched Mama leave the kitchen and commented to Bev, "She's doing much better, isn't she?"

"Yes, she is. I think she really appreciates you being back home, Rena."

I felt the same appreciation. Some days it surprised me given the number of years I'd stayed away.

Bev peeked inside the oven, and I glimpsed a rather large turkey.

I pointed towards the golden brown bird. "Mmm, looking good, Sis."

Bev's hair was pulled back into a ponytail, making her look way younger than her thirty-six years. I knew she'd been in the kitchen last night and this morning. "You must be tired. I'm not sure what help I can be, but I'm willing to be of assistance."

Bev smiled, "You can help set the table."

"Oh, so that's all I'm good at doing?"

Bev rolled her eyes. "Somebody has to do it and I know you can handle it."

With that, I grabbed Bev's good dishes, a China set passed down from Bev's paternal grandmother. I remembered Reverend Lawson's mother, but I didn't spend much time with her. Usually, when Bev visited with her dad's mom, I would be at Aunt C's. While we were sisters, the fact that we had separate dads often set us in two different worlds when we were younger.

I set up the table in the dining room, listening to the girls in the family room argue about something on television. Since it was right off the kitchen, I started to go around and ask the girls to help but decided I could handle the one task Bev gave me on my own. I heard the front doorbell ring, and a few seconds later, I glimpsed Clay heading past the dining room to the front door.

Wow, guests already? Most people knew to come through the side door into the kitchen.

I checked to make sure each place setting had all the utensils before I headed towards the kitchen. I heard voices, one very familiar one.

I stopped at the door and caught sight of Queen Bradley.

What almost knocked me over was the fact that Trey was standing right next to her.

My eyes locked with Trey's and then trailed to Queen, who had the usual smug look on her face that I was accustomed to. This woman and I didn't like each other from the very first time we met, mainly because I recognized her for what she truly was about. Trying to get her claws on the most eligible bachelor at Zion Baptist Church.

Minister Trey Evans.

I was reminded about my last face-to-face meeting with Trey. His jealousy over my spending time working with Amir. I guess the tables were turned today especially if Trey showed up at this house with *that* woman.

I turned away. The one thing I knew about myself, there was no way I could hide the look of pure disgust and hurt on my face.

Happy Thanksgiving!

Chapter Twenty-Five

Thanksgiving Day, 1:54 pm

Bev's face was alarmed like she did something horribly wrong, but I wasn't really in the mood to know what my sister had been thinking. It was her house, and she was the one hosting Thanksgiving. *What was there for me to say?*

I'm not sure what happened in the commotion of other people arriving and greeting each other, but I managed to completely ignore Queen, and Trey for that matter. Once the kitchen was rid of all its new guests, Bev came over to me, reaching for my arm. "I'm sorry, I forgot to tell you."

I crossed my arms, "Tell me what?"

Bev knew I'd butted heads a number of times with Queen. The woman didn't hold back that she didn't like me either. Despite being the perfect Christian woman, some of the snottiest things came out of her mouth.

Bev wrung her hands together, "I knew this time of the year would be hard for Queen. You know she lost her mother last year?"

I sighed. I couldn't get mad with my sister for doing something sweet. "I remember. Look, don't mind me.

You do your thing. Just let me know where else I can help."

Bev narrowed her eyes and leaned closer to me. "You know she didn't come with Trey, right?"

I raised an eyebrow, somehow feeling my mood lighten slightly. "Really?"

My sister nodded. "She arrived after he did. Trey showed up at the side door and was already in the kitchen." My sister's eyes darted behind me at the counter, "We were talking."

"Oh." I wasn't about to let my sister know how relieved I was to hear Trey hadn't arrived with Queen. That made sense that I didn't see him when he arrived, but why didn't he speak to me. Surely, Bev would have told him I was setting the table.

Bev went to check on the biscuits she'd placed in the oven before turning back to me. "Is there something going on between you and Trey? You both didn't speak to each other."

"You noticed?"

"Yes."

I watched Bev grab the mitts again. She bent down to pull out the pan of biscuits.

"That's Grandma Lawson's recipe?" I asked, hoping to change the subject.

Bev nodded, "Yes, I don't make these often, but today seemed like a good time." She glanced at me. "I know you don't want to talk about this now. Can you grab that basket over on the counter?"

I brought my sister the basket.

"Can you add the biscuits, cover them with the cloth and set them on the table?"

"Sure, I can handle that."

As I worked to arrange the biscuits in the basket, Bev stated, "You know Trey is worried about you."

"What?"

He came over the other night to talk to Clay. "I overheard him mention you have some young guy working on a case with you."

I rolled my eyes. *Really, Trey?* He was still going on about Amir. I wasn't sure how to feel at this point.

"Look, let's just eat. I don't want to talk about this now. I want to enjoy my day off."

Bev knew I was on edge, and she wasn't about to let me spoil her Thanksgiving meal, so she hushed up.

Soon, we were all seated around the table. Clay said grace, and then had the honor of slicing up the turkey. As the bowls of food went around the table, I forgot about the case, Trey, and Amir, soaking in the goodness of the meal. I'd given myself an extra heavy helping of macaroni and cheese and was enjoying the cheesy favorite when I realized someone was talking to me.

Queen.

Somehow I had missed that she was sitting next to Trey.

I tried my best to ignore how conveniently Queen decided to stay close to Trey. After all, Bev said this was a really hard time for her.

She looked across the table, "Sorry, I guess you didn't hear me. I asked how you like being a private investigator?"

I wasn't really in the mood to be talking. Eating was on my agenda, but I chose to be polite, "It's going great."

"I bet you get a lot of cheating spouses, huh?"

I glanced down at my brother-in-law, who grinned at me. I grinned back. "Well, sometimes Clay's clients file for divorce for those reasons."

"That's such a shame. Do you have to catch them in the act?"

I wasn't sure why Queen wanted to have this conversation right now. It wasn't like she cared about what I did for a living. I glanced at Trey, "Usually the spouse wants evidence."

Queen wriggled her body and turned up her nose. "I guess you must see really disgusting stuff."

I raised my eyebrow. Once again, I was puzzled by the purpose of this conversation. But I understood more clearly as I watched Queen look lovingly at Trey like he was all the man for her. The only problem was Trey was looking across the table at me, and I couldn't read his expression.

Queen's voice floated across the table again. "Weren't you a reporter too? I guess that's where you developed the skills to do all this private detective stuff."

I smiled, but I wasn't feeling the smile. I wanted this woman to stop talking to me.

Next to me, a noise made me jump. I turned to see Mama had knocked over her glass of iced tea. I reached for the glass before the liquid spread any further across the table.

Mama looked distraught.

I patted her hand, "Don't worry, I got it." Bev stood from where she sat, but I waved to her, giving my sister a pointed look. "Sit, you've been on your feet all day. I got this."

I don't know whether Mama intentionally or accidentally knocked her glass over, but she had just saved her oldest daughter from losing her cool. I was about two seconds from throwing my fork at Queen. And that wasn't the kind of thing I wanted to ask forgiveness for. It was bad enough the vision had just crossed my mind as Mama's drink spilled.

God works in mysterious ways.

I brought Mama back a glass of iced tea.

I don't know if anyone said anything to Queen, but I noticed she no longer had questions for me. I finished off my meal in peace without once looking up at her or Trey. After the meal was over, I helped clear the dishes off the table.

As I grabbed the last of the plates from the table, I turned to see someone helping me.

Trey.

"You don't have to do that. I thought I heard Clay watching a game. He could probably use some company."

"Probably, but we haven't said two words to each other and it's Thanksgiving."

"I guess that is kind of weird." I carried the dishes to the kitchen and proceeded to scrape the plates and then load them into the dishwasher. My sister was in the living room, I suspected with Queen.

Trey followed me into the kitchen, so we were alone.

"How have you been this week? Making any headway on your cases?"

I responded politely, "Slow, but steady." I remembered I wanted to make a plate for Amir, but then got self-conscious about doing so with Trey standing there.

"I'm sorry."

I turned and looked at Trey. "Why the apology?"

"About last week. I shouldn't have gotten upset."

"No, you shouldn't have. I mean you have..." I started to say something not very nice about Queen but thought better of it.

Trey grinned. "I know what you were about to say."

I narrowed my eyes. "Do you?"

"Let's just say I can relate to how you're feeling. There's definitely nothing going on between me and Queen."

"Mmmm, you may want to tell her that. And you don't need to share your worries about Amir with my family. I'm a big girl, Trey. I told you we were working together professionally." I stretched out the words, hoping to add emphasis.

"I know that. I just don't want to see you hurt, Rena."

I nodded. "I appreciate your concern." I couldn't help but wink. "I know you're used to being the main man in my life."

He lifted his eyes as if asking help from God and then stepped forward. "I promise you I'm not jealous, I'm just wondering how much you know about him in such a short time period."

I sighed, "I have a sense for people's demeanors, Trey. I've interviewed and been around tons of people in my life, both good and bad, and I *can* tell when something isn't right about a person."

He placed his hands on my shoulders. "If you feel like you can trust him, then I trust your instincts. But know this, I'm going to pray for you anyway. You're walking a path that God has for you with this private investigator career. I know that, even if I come off like a jerk."

I smiled, my eyes were brimming with unshed tears that seemed to appear out of nowhere, "Being a jerk is not possible for you. I know you mean well, Trey. You have always been a good guy."

"Thank you, Rena. Don't forget to include God in everything you do. I know God will protect you. I guess I need to remind myself of that too."

Trey pulled me to him, wrapping me up in a real bear hug.

After he left the kitchen, I stood there still feeling the imprint of his arms around me and wiped the moisture from my eyes. I already had plenty to be thankful for, but until this moment, it never occurred to me that a man who prays for you would be one of them.

That was something I'd never experienced before.

Lord, thank you.

Chapter Twenty-Six

Thanksgiving Day, 5:20 pm

I was still in a daze when I dropped Mama off. I turned to say goodbye, and she greeted me with a lopsided grin.

"What? Why are you smiling like that?"

Mama shook her head. "I know that look. I hope you and Trey made up. You need someone in your life, Rena." With that, Mama opened the passenger car door and stepped out. Not giving me time to respond, she closed the door and headed up the walkway to her house.

I couldn't help but smile. It was kind of nice to know my family recognized my feelings for Trey. Even better that Trey knew I had feelings for him too. All those years ago when he seemed to be clueless about my feelings for him, I suffered in silence.

After I saw Mama enter her house safely, I turned the car around to head in the opposite direction of my house. I hadn't mentioned to anyone that one of the plates I filled with Bev's cooking was for Amir. *Why do I feel guilty?* Amir had information, and I knew he'd been alone most of the day. It seemed like the right thing to do.

Just like my sister deciding to invite Queen Bradley to Thanksgiving, right?

Amir's house was a modest ranch-style brick home. He drove a late model black Mustang, which I hadn't really seen until now. Somehow the muscle car matched Amir's personality. He was no doubt a geek, but not the *Revenge of the Nerds* kind of geek. Like most web tycoons, he was good-looking and charismatic.

It took Amir a few seconds to answer after I knocked on the door. He greeted me in a black hoodie and loose gray pants with a smile that warmed me.

"Hey, thanks for coming by. I thought for sure you would be enjoying your family the rest of the day."

"I had enough of them for the day." I raised the white grocery bag so he could see it, "But I brought you some goodies."

His eyes widened, almost reminding me of a kid who hit the jackpot at Christmas time.

"Thank you. You didn't have to do that, but I appreciate it. Come in."

I entered his house expecting a college dorm look but was surprised to see the pleasant decor. Dark hardwood flooring reached all the way back into an open area that included sleek black leather couches and chairs. The focus of the room was a massive flat screen television attached to the wall. Below the television were black bookcases with an array of game controllers and VR goggles. The walls were decked out with elegant black-framed superheroes. *Okay, now this is definitely a guy pad. I like it.*

I raised my eyebrow, feeling a toothy grin spread across my face. "Marvel Avengers fan, I see."

Amir grinned sheepishly, once again reminding me of a young boy.

Compared to Trey, not that I was into comparisons, Amir really was a boy. His tastes were pretty similar to Joseph, just more sophisticated.

I followed him back to a kitchen that any chef would envy. There were stainless steel appliances all around. *Okay, not so boyish.*

"Would you like anything to drink? I can make some coffee."

I approached a breakfast nook in the corner and sat down. "Coffee would be good."

While the coffee brewed, Amir sat and relished the plate of Thanksgiving leftovers. I turned my attention outside the window to the wooden lounge chairs and large gas grill on his patio deck. I wondered how often Amir had people over to his house and who. I'm sure if Samantha were alive, she would have been here at his house for Thanksgiving.

He got up to fix a cup of coffee for me.

"Sugar? Cream?"

"Yes, two spoons of sugar and cream. Thanks."

We continued in a comfortable silence until Amir leaned back with his hand on his stomach. "Wow, I don't remember the last time I had a homecooked meal like that."

I glanced around his kitchen. "With this kitchen, looks like you can throw down yourself. Have you ever had anyone over to your house for the holidays?"

"The first year I moved in, I hosted Thanksgiving. Samantha was here. We invited a few friends over that weren't heading home to be with family. It was a good day. I didn't do too bad with the turkey." He smiled, his eyes focusing on his memory. "Samantha made potato salad. I forgot where she got the recipe, but it was the best."

"Wow. Sounds like you're quite the cook."

He smirked, "I try. Most days, I usually eat out more than I'd like to admit. Tell your sister I appreciate the food. She's a really good cook."

"Better you experience her cooking than mine. I couldn't cook like this ever."

He studied me. "So, you want to head to my office? I have something that will really shed some light on Edwin's activities."

I was tired from the day's eating and other events. "Let me finish this coffee. You can clue me in on what you found and if you think it's what Judith needs."

He sat back. "I think what I found will be more than enough. And to be honest, Judith may have second thoughts about what she asked."

I swallowed my coffee so fast it went down the wrong windpipe, and I spent the next minute hacking. "Sorry, you kind of triggered a reaction there. I'm not sure I'm prepared to see what you found."

He looked down at the table. "Let's just say it's been eye-opening. I think I discovered the errands that Samantha had been doing for Edwin too."

I stared at him. The tightness in his face, as if he was holding back anger, spoke volumes to me. "It's not good?"

"It's something I would have never imagined."

"Let's go. Show me what you got."

Amir took me to his office which was more like a high level tech room. The room appeared to have been a former bedroom that included a desk with two large screen monitors. Across from the desk was a wall that included a large screen television and a few other smaller monitors.

"You must have a serious electric and internet bill."

Amir laughed, "That I do. But I can get what I need done in my office."

I walked around the room checking out the monitors on the wall. It took me a few moments to realize they were hooked to surveillance cameras outside. One camera was directed to the front of the house, showing my car next to Amir's car in the driveway. The other cameras seemed to be pointed to what was the back and sides of the house. I turned to Amir, my mouth opened. "Nobody is sneaking past you. This is a serious surveillance setup."

Amir's smile was tight. "It's set to my house for now, but I can see other locations."

I stared at him, afraid to speak. "You mean you can tap into other cameras?"

"Most with permission. I monitor some of my client's properties when they're not there."

"Some cameras, you may not have permission?"

Amir raised his eyebrow. "I don't want to make you nervous, Rena. I do what my client's need me to do. It's best me and you stick to the case on hand."

I'd had some doubts between listening to Trey and Moses about Amir, but now I was starting to wonder how star struck I'd been about him. "So, how were you able to get past the IT guy at Waterway or is that something you don't want me to know either?"

He smiled, "I sweet talked Irma into getting some passwords."

My mouth dropped open again. "No, you didn't. She shared Edwin's passwords?"

"She's his secretary. Irma knows everything. And I might add, she doesn't like him very much."

"I got that impression too. Still, you trust her not to say anything if she's questioned later?"

"I do, and besides, I didn't tell her I was searching for information on her boss. I told her it was time for some upgrades to the system." He winked, "Very legitimate reason to get admin privileges."

"I thought I was bold, but you youngin' are way too bold for me."

He grinned. "Oh, I'm a youngin' now?"

"Yes, you're considerably younger than me."

"If I was older, would I get a chance?"

I stared at him, my face on fire. But before I could answer, he said, "Never mind, I could tell Minster Trey Evans has your heart. He might be a minister, but I believe he'd put up a fight for you."

This conversation was not cooling me off at all. "Really?" I squelched, feeling radioactive heat. *I sound like a little girl.*

Amir shrugged, "Guys are territorial. In his own way, *your friend* marked his territory the other day in your office."

I laughed, "That's funny."

"But it's true. He's a lucky guy." Amir pulled out a chair and rolled it beside him. "Have a seat. It will take me a minute to tap back into the system."

I watched as Amir's fingers fluttered over the keyboard typing in characters that I had no clue about in a black window that appeared in the corner of one of the monitors.

"There we go."

I leaned forward as Amir zoned in on what looked like some ratty building within a strip mall. Then the screen filled with several hole-in-the wall type buildings. "What's this? Please don't tell me these are potential real estate properties."

"No, these are separate business ventures that feed into Waterway or at least provide income to Edwin."

"What are you talking about? These look like strip joints."

He nodded, "A very profitable business, especially in a state where tourism is a billion dollar industry."

"How are you seeing these connected to Edwin?"

"Remember I told you the other day about the company that is apparently listed under his son's name? Well, that company is essentially a shell company—"

"A shell company?" I interrupted.

"Yes, these types of companies are inactive, and many times they're used to push money around. A lot of times these companies remain dormant for some future use. Knowing that, I decided to dig deeper. Suppose there are other shell companies..." Amir turned back to the screen and pulled up some documents.

I leaned closer as he opened several PDFs.

His hands flew across the keyboard. "I was right. I found a paper trail that's not obvious. It's actually rather hidden in correspondence. What caught my attention was the fact that these LLC documents were drafted by a very high-profile attorney out of Atlanta who has some interesting clientele. I'm sure Edwin didn't mean for this to be seen, but I was able to restore these artifacts from his drive.

I frowned, trying to wrap my head around what Amir was saying. "So, that's like when you think you deleted something on your computer or online, but it's not really gone?"

"Bingo. You got it."

I briefly scanned the documents on the monitor. "These are all companies owned by Edwin?"

"Yes, Edwin ultimately owns these buildings. He's the landlord, and there is no way he doesn't get passed any money that is transacted."

"Illegal transactions? Drugs maybe?"

"Could be, but I haven't been able to make any drug or drug dealer connections." He sighed, his face grim. "But I'm pretty sure the girls who work at these places are a different story."

My eyes grew wide. "They're more than just strippers? Or, wait, I think most prefer the term exotic dancer."

He chuckled for a minute and then grew somber. "I think this is where Sam did her errands."

I balked, "Stripping? No way. She was a pretty girl, but there was a dignity about her."

"No, more like an escort girl." Amir pulled up a few photos.

I peered at the photos of an elegantly dressed woman wearing a tight white shimmering dress. She wore gold slingback heels. It took me a moment to recognize her face with the heavy makeup, but the woman was no doubt Samantha. I looked at Amir. "How did you find this?"

Amir's eyes were red, his anger barely contained as he stared at the photo. "This photo, along with other photos, was found on Edwin's drive too. Looks like he took them with his phone. They were stored in the cloud." He shook his head. "Anyway, most of these photos show girls similar in age to Sam. I started to wonder about the ethnicity of some of the women. They didn't look like they were from around here."

"Human trafficking," I whispered. Goosebumps rose on my arms, though I knew the temperature hadn't changed in the office.

Amir's phone chirped breaking the solemn silence that had settled between us. He looked at his phone but chose to ignore it.

I swallowed, "I still can't wrap my head around this. Edwin has a daughter this age."

Amir's nostrils flared, "But yet he liked to leer at her best friend."

His phone chirped again.

"Do you want to answer your phone?"

He shook his head, "No, it's just Janine."

That surprised me. "Really, are you sure you should just ignore Samantha's best friend?"

Amir grimaced, "I understand she's grieving. I am too. She's just too clingy right now. I'm grieving Sam in my own way." He pushed his chair back as though he needed space. "Besides, it's kind of awkward right now. Look at what I've found on her father. I can't even face her."

"Good point. Sounds like you're doing the right thing." I turned back to the photos littered across the screen. "We can certainly make a case to give to the police, but can we? I mean how would you explain where you obtained all of this. Back during my reporter days, I had my sources. I'm not sure I could get away with that now as a P.I."

"I'm sure we can figure out something. Who says we should go to the police first? Do you trust them?"

I frowned, "What do you mean?"

Amir scoffed, "It's a known fact that folks in high places have their hands in Edwin's pockets." He swung his chair back to the desk and swiftly ran his hands back over the keyboard. Another set of photos popped up. "Here's Edwin in the center. On this side is the chief of police and this guy is the mayor."

Amir tapped his keyboard again, "Here are both of these guys. Look at the women. Definitely the same event, but do you think the women on their arms are their wives?"

I shook my head. "Where were these photos taken? It's looks a lot classier than the hole-in-the-walls you showed me."

"It is. From what I was able to gather from the photo metadata, this is a high rise condo on Myrtle Beach, where high rollers frequent."

Another slight chill passed over me. "You're right, Judith didn't know what she was asking us to do. I think it's best to show her what you have and let her decide. It's what she hired us to do."

Amir looked at me. "Suppose she changes her mind?"

"We can't do anything about that, Amir."

"But you see what he had Sam doing, right?" No longer able to contain his emotions, Amir stood sending the chair flying backwards.

I was startled by his outburst but remained calm. It was amazing to me that he hadn't already let loose his anger. "I'm sorry that you saw these, Amir."

He turned to me. "Sam didn't do this willingly. That person wasn't her. She was sweet and kind. If she was supposed to be like a daughter to him, and if he was so fond of her mother, why would he have her involved in this filthy mess?"

I shook my head. I didn't know Samantha, but I felt my emotions wavering too. If we took this to Judith, what would she do with it? I hated to admit it, but maybe Amir and I needed to get this information out. It was so much bigger than I'd imagined.

I didn't have time to think about it. Suddenly, alarms clanged. I held my hands over my ears, while Amir whirled towards his monitors on the wall. In the next few minutes, he was out the door.

Still with my hand over my ears, I walked to the monitor. I could clearly see a figure in black almost blending in the darkness. The figure took off, away from the camera. A few seconds later, Amir showed up in the camera monitor.

I sucked in my breath, forgetting the sirens blaring in my ear.

Amir was holding out a gun. Where did that gun come from?

I couldn't hear the gunshot, but I saw the spark from where I stood.

Chapter Twenty-Seven

Thanksgiving Day, 6:06 pm

I held my hand to my chest and continued to watch Amir on the monitors as he ran from the side of the house to the backyard. My heart felt as if it would burst through my chest. I didn't want to see anything happen to Amir. I wasn't sure if I could take it since I'd been so consumed with Samantha. I didn't know either of these young people, but they both had become a part of my life the past few weeks. On the monitor, Amir burst on the screen in a full sprint around to the front of the house.

Did he shoot the figure? Whoever was out there seemed to be long gone now. But were they running away bleeding? There would be no way to see evidence in the dark. Still, I wondered who the figure was. Did their presence have anything to do with Amir's tapping into Edwin's network? Did Amir create his own digital footprint and trigger some alarm?

All of these questions raced through my mind before I realized the alarms had stopped ringing in my ears. I searched the monitors; I couldn't see Amir on the cameras anymore. He must have entered the house.

"Rena, are you okay?"

I spun around to see Amir removing the magazine from his gun, which appeared to be a Glock. His face was shiny with sweat and his chest was heaving. He stood with a stance that suggested he was ready to fly back outside again.

"Yeah, I'm fine. I was worried about you." My eyes zoned in on the gun his hand. This man was full of surprises. "You do have a license for that, right?"

He smirked, "Yes. A man has a right to protect his property. As you can see by my unexpected visitor."

I held up my hands in defense. "No problem, I agree." I stepped towards him, my eyes straying to the Glock in his hands. "Do you think your figure in black has something to do with Edwin?"

Amir shook his head. He walked over behind the desk and placed the Glock on the desk. "No, I'm pretty sure Edwin has no idea what I've dug up on him."

I turned to watch him. Still something about his face made me nervous. "So you have no idea who that was outside?"

He rubbed his hand across his head. "Not a clue, but I'm going to have cops at my door." He looked at the screen. "Right on time. I need to go deal with them. Do you mind hanging out here for a while longer? I know we talked about giving this info to Judith, I just I have reservations about trusting her to do anything with it."

On the monitor, I watched a cop climb out of the Georgetown County police cruiser. I nodded, "Sure, go take care of the cops. I will hang out here so we can talk."

I rushed around behind the desk after Amir walked out. I really wanted to take a closer look at the figure. From my brief view, the figure in black had a tall slim build. If Edwin was behind this, I pictured him sending a muscle man or even more than one guy to take care of Amir.

I stared down at Amir's desk setup, I knew there had to be some way to the view surveillance camera footage. But I didn't have any idea how to work the computer, and the photos that were on the screen moments before the intruder showed up were now hidden. Amir's obsession with Marvel's Avengers was apparent from his screensaver. The iconic poster image from *Infinity War* showing Thanos at the top with the large cast of characters including Iron Man, Black Widow, Thor, Captain America, Black Panther, and the cast from *Guardians of the Galaxy*. I clicked the mouse, and then the keyboard hoping the photos would appear again. Instead, I was met with a login screen.

I sucked in a breath. I wouldn't expect anything less from a computer expert.

Not sure of what else to do with myself, I sat down in the chair. Amir's Glock sat only inches from my hand. Once again, I was reminded of other people's concerns about me getting too close to this guy. I really didn't know anything about the man other than he'd just lost one of his best friends, a girl who was like family. A girl who'd been exposed to the shady part of life…by a really dirty guy.

I was with Amir. We had to expose Edwin Peters no matter the consequences.

From where I sat, by the looks of the office, I had to wonder about Amir's life. Was all of this equipment, even the Glock, really for his cybersecurity business? How did he know how to look in all the right places to dig up dirt on Edwin Peters?

I ran my hands across the desk. Unlike my desktop, it was free of dust bunnies. Organization wasn't my strong suit, but Amir kept his papers neat and orderly in a tray on the side of his desk. My eyes strayed to a manila envelope peeking out from a stack. It seemed to be calling for me to pull it out. Okay, maybe it wasn't calling to me, but I couldn't help but reach for it. Unlike the other carefully arranged items, it was sticking out like it had been shoved.

I looked at the door expecting Amir to return at any second. I imagined the cop had many questions. Amir purposely kept his gun in the office which I'm sure he didn't want to get into with the cop. From what I could see on the monitor, Amir shot at least one round. Hopefully, no one reported it.

The yellow envelope was in my hand, and I found myself carefully twirling the string that closed the envelope. There was paper inside. Photo paper. I pulled out the photos thinking maybe they were related to what Amir showed me on the screen. I sucked in a breath.

No, no, these were the photos I'd taken with my own camera.

The photos of Samantha when she was at Edwin's house had been destroyed. I'd destroyed them myself.

Amir was never to see these photos. Apparently, I had a lot to learn about a man who knew his way around the digital world.

Chapter Twenty-Eight

Thanksgiving Day - 7:11 pm

Confused, I paced the room until Amir finished with the cop. Amir seemed like a good guy on the surface, but I was wondering if I should trust him. The man had access to photos that I'd destroyed. Only Judith and I had copies, and I'm pretty sure Judith destroyed her copies since it was her request. I was thrilled an hour ago with what Amir had dug up on Edwin, but how borderline creepy it was that this young man could dig into someone's life was unsettling to my stomach.

Detective Moses' dropped comments about Amir's past illegal activities and now the information he was able to obtain in the past week was making me paranoid. I looked around his room thinking it resembled something at the Pentagon or something. Maybe Trey's worries were getting to me now.

Knowing Amir had researched me and knew about my past career, I wanted to know how much Amir had dug up on me. Not that my past was squeaky clean, but I'd always kept my quest for my stories as clean as possible. I did cross lines occasionally if it helped me publish the truth. Someone like Amir, who could find information, would become my protected source.

I was starting to get a headache. The kind I get when I'm upset. I turned back to the desk, my eyes falling on the photos that I'd decided to leave out in the open.

Amir appeared in the doorway, "That was an ordeal."

I didn't wait to ask him how things went with the cop. The almost break-in was more of an afterthought as I pointed to the desk. "How did you get these?"

Amir walked around behind the desk, stared at me and then reached for the photos and the envelope. He began stuffing the photos back into the envelope as if he didn't want to see them.

Before I realized I was going to do it, I grabbed his arm. "Judith asked me to destroy these. How do you still have copies?"

Amir looked down at my hand on his arm.

I quickly let go and stepped back from the desk. *Not smart, Rena.*

He frowned, "Judith asked you to destroy these? Why?"

"She didn't want Janine or Ethan to see them. Instead, she hired me to work with you to go after Edwin." I pointed to the envelope that Amir was quickly closing back. "These came from my assignment the night Samantha was killed. I captured these photos at the house in Pawleys Island. Judith was devastated when she saw these the next day. She wanted to catch Edwin with some floozy, but not with Samantha. How did you get these?"

Amir sat down hard in the chair behind him, enough to make it roll back. "I had no idea those photos existed until this week. When Judith asked me to scan the servers, that also included their personal computers. I needed to check what Edwin may have stored away from the office."

I frowned. "You found these photos on a computer in their home? No way. I gave Judith printouts. No one had digital copies except me."

He looked at me. "Are you sure?"

"Yes, I destroyed what was on my camera. I even checked my cloud storage. I never sent those photos electronically anywhere." I got heated. "Did you hack my computer?"

He jumped up, "No, I wouldn't do that. Besides, when did you delete them?"

"I called myself deleting them the morning before you came to my office." I paced the room. "Of course, I know geeks like you will say nothing is ever really removed."

Amir held up his hands. "I promise you, those copies came off a computer in the Peters' home."

I snatched the envelope off his desk and pulled the photos out again. I stared at them, not really seeing the scenes that were already embedded in my mind. Amir came up behind me. The more I studied the paper in my hand, the more I realized there was something different. "These don't look like the originals."

"No, they look like someone took a picture of the hard copies Judith had."

"So, you found these on a computer in the Peters' home? Would it be a computer they all used?"

He nodded. "Possibly. There's a desktop in the family room and in the office. I know everyone has their own laptops too."

"Do photos have a footprint, what you guys call metadata, to the original source? Is that how you were able to track information from the photos you found on Edwin's drive or cloud space?"

"Yeah, I can trace that information. There's A.I. technology or artificial intelligence now that Google, Amazon … all of these search engines can extract data like location of a photo. Cameras like yours store all that information."

I shook my head. "This is not good. I need to talk to Judith."

Amir studied my face, "About what I've found on Edwin? That's more important."

"You're right. What you uncovered is a lot more serious." I looked at Amir, we stood face to face, well almost, he had a few inches on me so his head was tilted towards mine. I stepped back again replacing the photos on the desk. "I jumped on you about those photos, but I haven't asked what you really thought about them."

His face was blank.

I assumed he thought a whole lot about them. "I imagine seeing those is why you went extra hard this week, even sweet talking Irma, to extract the data from Waterway's servers."

He looked at me. "Sam didn't deserve that. Edwin had no business putting his hands on her. I always thought he was a perv. Those photos just prove it. I know Judith wanted you to destroy them, but she had no right to ask you to do that. Sam's not here to defend herself. Someone did kill her, Rena."

"You're right," I said quietly. "Judith's reasons were selfish, she didn't want Janine or Ethan to find out. But... we have a lot worse information on their dad. Judith seemed pretty okay with us going after him. She seemed to sense his hands were dirty about something."

Amir's voice broke, his eyes focused on the desk, that envelope. "I kept asking Sam, 'Why do you go to him? He's not your father.' She would say he has errands for me to run in exchange for money." The rawness of his emotions made his voice tremble. "Was that an errand too?"

I swallowed, not knowing how to respond. "He's a monster, and he will get punished. Even if it's not for Samantha, Edwin will get what's coming to him."

I looked around the room. "Do you have a shredder?"

He glowered at me, "Yes."

"Please destroy these. Get rid of the electronic versions. Don't keep these around. Samantha was obviously in some duress over her decisions. Be her friend in death. She was a victim. Don't leave these around."

He reached out slowly and took the envelope, twisting it between his hands. "These images won't ever leave my mind."

"I know. Now you see how I've been feeling the past few weeks." I started to walk away, but then turned around abruptly. "You know what? I hate to do this but see if you can find the footprint of the electronic copy.

Maybe we shouldn't destroy them yet. Something tells me that's going to be key to who killed Samantha."

His eyes grew wide. "You think someone in the Peters' house killed Sam?"

"Just dig and see what you can find. I expected Judith to have destroyed these before me." I walked over and grabbed his shoulders. "Let me talk to Judith. Don't do anything rash. You're sitting on a powder keg, and we still don't know who that was sneaking around your house."

"Don't worry. I'm good." He frowned. "You be careful too, Rena. Your car was seen at my house."

That thought had crossed my mind, but I didn't want to linger.

I walked back towards my car, glimpsing the side of the house for where I thought the camera had caught the person trying to break into the house. I wondered what that person thought they would find. How did they know to find Amir?

Amir seemed to think Edwin wasn't on to his snooping in the company's computer network. The figure who tried to break in didn't seem like some heavy duty muscle man. Maybe I'd watched too many crime shows myself.

As a former reporter, I dealt with facts. The one thing I always did was dot every "I" and cross every "T." They wouldn't be happy, but it was time for me to check-in with my friendly neighborhood detectives.

Chapter Twenty-Nine

Friday, November 23, Black Friday, 6:03 am

Thanksgiving Day was long and a lot more adventurous than I could have ever imagined. Despite my anxiety over the events at Amir's house, I was too exhausted to do anything but sleep. I was too old for that kind of excitement. I needed the rest. When I awoke, the sun had not yet risen but I was not one of those die hard Black Friday shoppers.

My mind spun with all the information Amir found on Edwin Peters. That creep was even worse than I'd imagined. Living in his million dollar homes, walking around like a real estate tycoon, Edwin may not have been directly involved in what went on in his seedier establishments, but he had to be raking in money. Money that exploited young girls and women. Young girls like poor Samantha. Not to include, young like the own man's daughter.

What really bothered me was the fact that Edwin was a father. He certainly wasn't fatherly, which made my suspicions about what kind of man he was at home rise.

I tore myself from the warmth of the bed, wondering about Judith. How could she have been around this man for so long and not know? Women, deep down, knew when something wasn't right about their partner. She knew Edwin wasn't faithful. In fact, Judith knew Edwin's income wasn't all legal. How? What had the woman seen?

Amir was right. We couldn't completely trust Judith with the information he dug up. Not when she wanted to protect her children. Heading to the bathroom, I almost tripped over the cat as a word popped in my mind.

Self-preservation.

An educator and school principal. The descendent of a wealthy southern family. Judith was the epitome of an elegant Southern belle. Her head had been in the sand for years, now she wanted to separate herself completely from Edwin Peters with this divorce.

I brushed my teeth, staring at my reflection in the mirror. My eyes were a bit puffy from sleep, but I was alert. My skin tingled with the anticipation. I hadn't felt like this in a long time. Well, since last year when I poked my nose in another murder investigation.

Lord, I'm close to something. I believe there is even more to come. I'm praying I don't get myself into trouble. Please protect me. Protect Amir too.

Amir was like a quiet ticking bomb. I hoped Amir wouldn't go off the tracks himself with what he knew. His anger simmered, and despite his ignorance about who was at his house last night, the presence ignited the danger that Amir was no doubt used to. What other clients did he work for and what did he do for them?

I managed to feed the cat, run my own coffee maker, down a cup and stuff some toast in my mouth before leaving the house.

Both detectives appeared shaved and rested when I showed up at their desks. "Looks like you both enjoyed your Thanksgiving."

Moses sneered at me. "Shouldn't you be out shopping, catching some Black Friday deals?"

I quipped, "That was way too early for me this morning. Plus, I'm a one-click online shopper. Nothing like the sight of packages or the man in the brown uniform at my door."

Moses rolled his eyes.

I pulled up a seat. "Questions for you."

Moses interrupted, "Let me guess, you want to check to see if your new friend, Amir is still on our list."

I smiled, "He has a definite alibi, but my question is about the Peters."

Baldwin stretched his long arms over his head and yawned, "Which one? Edwin's alibi has checked out."

"And Judith's alibi was supported by her son." I raised my eyebrow. "A thirteen-year old. Really, guys?"

Moses responded, "Actually, three thirteen year olds confirmed Judith's alibi."

I raised an eyebrow, "What?"

Moses rubbed his jaw, " Erin Peters had two classmates spend the night. Mrs. Peters was at home making homemade pizza. She was being mama and chaperone the night Samantha was killed."

I nodded, "And Janine?"

Moses looked at me quizzically. "The best friend?"

"Why not? You still claim to have her other best friend on your suspect list."

Moses rolled his head back, lifting his eyes to the heavens, I supposed.

Baldwin chuckled, "Janine was at school. She goes to Furman in Greenville."

I shot back, "Which is about a four hour trip to Georgetown. Are you sure she was in Greenville?"

Moses frowned, "Yes, we checked with her roommate and another friend on campus."

I whipped out my phone. "You care to share the roommate and friend's name?"

Baldwin and Moses both stared at me. Baldwin, in his nice way, gave me a grin to appease me. "What are you doing, Rena? I'm with Moses on this one. Why don't you back off and let us handle this?"

If only these two knew the information about Edwin that I was sitting on. There was still so much I was piecing together, but I was fairly certain someone close to Samantha was in that apartment. Maybe they didn't intend to kill her, but they found out something that set them off to rage against the young woman. If these guys didn't want to share any more information, I would certainly find out. "Okay, I just have one more question. What kind of vehicles do the Peters' drive?"

"Why do you need to know?" Moses asked.

"Look, I'm here to help you. Do you want to close this case? Since you showed up at my house, then you know I was one of the last people to see Samantha Livingston alive. You also know I was staking out the place she had to run from with her life. What if there is something I saw, but I'm missing?"

Both detectives looked at each other. Baldwin asked, "Did you see anyone else?"

I sighed. "A car passed me when the police cruiser showed up. You said a neighbor saw the police cruiser so that means there were other people around in the neighborhood that night."

Baldwin shrugged, while Moses conceded and flipped open his notebook. "Judith owns a 2015 BMW 535i. We told you Janine was at school, her 2016 Nissan Murano was at school. Edwin drives a 2018 Audi S6, which was parked at the house in Pawleys Island."

I quickly jotted the car info in the notes app on my phone. Then I looked up, "Okay."

Moses raised an eyebrow, "That's it?"

I started to shake my head, but then I thought about my last request. "Did you ever find a diary or calendar that Samantha used?"

Both detectives eyed me again. Baldwin tapped something on his machine, "The only thing we found, or rather, the techs found was on her laptop. She did keep an elaborate calendar. I guess it's a Google Calendar. The tech thought it had to do with her social media activities. The girl practically lived on Instagram every day. We've been observing interactions with her on social media too."

I nodded. "She had a ton of followers. Still, you guys are looking at the obvious, right? Who were the closest people to Samantha? Who would have been the most hurt or devastated by knowing she was with Edwin? What would be their first reaction?"

Moses opened his mouth, but I cut him off before he said anything, "It's not Amir. You're a guy. Who would you go after if you knew some man was messing with a young woman you were close to?"

Moses' shoulders slumped, "I would go after the other guy."

I saluted both men and then walked out. Deputy Wilson wasn't at the desk. As soon as I was in my Honda, I whipped out my phone and pressed Amir's number which was now officially listed on my speed dial list.

"Hey, Rena, what's up?"

"I probably shouldn't be asking you this, but do you have access to Samantha's Google account. I think the detectives stumbled upon something on her calendar but aren't sure what to do with it."

"Yes, I can probably get in. What do you think Sam had on her calendar?"

"Mainly her social media strategy from what they saw, but I have a feeling she kept more. Maybe her errands. Those would be more like appointments. I know I use mine to help me track what clients I'm on assignment for during the week."

"I see. I'll check it out. Where are you headed now?"

"I think it's time to reach out to Judith."

Amir was silent for a few seconds. "Are you going to tell her?"

"I'm going to tell her you've found some potentially devastating information and that we don't think we can just sit on it. Is there a way you can deliver it to her so she can view what you have?"

"I have been working on packaging up the content to protect it."

I frowned, "To protect it? How come I don't like the sound of that?"

"I'm just being cautious. If something happens," he cleared his throat, "I like to make sure copies can be found and are sent to the proper people."

My face grew warm. I looked around my car, examining the cars in the parking lot. I was at a police station so being paranoid felt a bit silly, but it still didn't help my discomfort. I swallowed, "You mean like something happening to you? Or us? Nothing is going to happen. Don't go there."

I couldn't see his face, but I could almost hear the smile in his voice. "Of course not. We got this, partner. Still, be careful."

"You too, Amir."

I ended the connection on my phone. I was still feeling uneasy and had a feeling my day was going to go downhill after my next visit.

I prayed.

Chapter Thirty

Black Friday - 7:12 pm

I didn't head to the Peters' home right away. I wanted to give Amir time to send what I needed Judith to see. I also wanted to do a bit of digging. Sure to his word, Amir sent me access to Samantha's Google account. It felt weird traipsing through her emails and her calendar, but I was learning more about her. I discovered that Samantha's potential errands were not that often, usually once every few months.

I was able to deduce the last time Samantha had trouble with the rent, she'd placed DATE NIGHT on her calendar. I was making a lot of assumptions that this date night wasn't with someone her age, mainly arriving at this conclusion based on details Samantha had listed including the location. These were no ordinary locations for a broke twenty year old, and a man Samantha's age couldn't afford these restaurants. The date had to be someone considerably older with money.

What I found really interesting was she had one of these date nights scheduled the Saturday after her death. Which made me wonder if her altercation with Edwin had to do with the fact that she didn't want to be pimped out in exchange for rent money anymore.

Digging through Samantha's emails, I also found some helpful information. Almost disturbing, in fact. There were quite a few emails back and forth with Janine, and the last correspondence was a whopper. I couldn't understand why the detective's tech guy didn't find this. According to the email, Janine told Samantha that she was dropping out of Furman and wanted to know if she could stay with her. Cherry's observation, 'Janine was jealous of Samantha' came to mind. *What was the friendship like between these two young women?* From this email, Janine leaned on Samantha as a friend who could offer her a place to stay.

There was a lot more missing in context from the emails. Like most young people, I assumed Samantha and Janine communicated more with texts or messenger. Without having access to Samantha's phone, I felt like I'd missed some valuable conversations between the two friends.

I noted this email was sent in October, approximately five weeks ago. If Janine had dropped out of school, where was she staying now? Had she come home anyway? Who was this supposed college roommate and friend providing Janine an alibi? That's what really didn't make sense.

I needed to touch base with Moses and Baldwin again, but first it was time to head back to the Peters' family home. I was itching to have a long overdue conversation with Janine as well as her mother.

I didn't notice it before, but off to the right was a two-car garage. I walked over and peeked in. A BMW was inside. I couldn't see it from the side, but the shape resembled the car that passed me that night on Pawleys Island. Of course, it was entirely possible the BMW that night belonged to a neighbor, and I was stretching a bit in my desperation to find out who killed Samantha.

I had an idea of what a Nissan Murano looked like, but I didn't see any signs of the SUV in the garage. Did that mean Janine wasn't home? She was the one I really wanted to talk to about her friend. Up until this point, what I knew about Janine, I'd only heard from other people. The two times I saw her, she was obviously grieving and distraught over the loss of her friend.

I rang the doorbell. I didn't tell Judith I was coming and hoped by now she'd received Amir's package, which he mentioned he would have delivered.

Judith's voice was strained as she called out through the loudspeaker next to the door, "Who is it?"

"It's Serena Manchester. I wanted to talk."

I looked around as I heard various locks being disengaged on the inside. I stepped inside, but my eyes had to adjust to the dark foyer.

Judith closed the door, "You should have called." She sounded as if she was having a hard time breathing through her nose.

"I'm sorry, it was fairly urgent that I speak to you." I narrowed my eyes, straining to see her face in the dim light that came through the windows of the front foyer. "Is this a bad time?"

"No, you're here. Let's walk back to the office. Amir sent me a package, but I haven't opened it. Is it about that?"

I started to nod my head, but realized I was facing her back. "It is."

I followed down a dim hallway that was lit by a cute night light. Inside the office, I welcomed the warm lighting supplied by a floor lamp in one corner and a lamp on the massive desk. It was then I noticed the bruise on Judith's face.

Now I see why it's so dark in the house.

Like some child, I pointed to her face. "Wow, what happened to you?"

Judith grimaced, and then shut her eyes as if she was in pain. "I'm a bit clumsy. I fell this morning. I was lying down before you came."

I knew Edwin had a temper from his assault on Samantha, now my curiosity was really piqued. "Should you go to the hospital? Has Edwin been here recently?"

Judith shook her head. "No, I'm fine. Edwin hasn't been back to the house since he moved out."

I narrowed my eyes, "Was he abusive too? That would be an even better reason to divorce him, Judith."

Judith didn't answer. She stared down at the desk.

I prodded her with another question, one I knew she had to answer. "Did he touch or hurt the kids?" I knew women who took a lot from their abuser, but their children was another story.

A sound came from Judith that sounded more like a whine than words.

I think I was starting to get the picture. I kept wondering why Edwin could be so despicable to Samantha, but the real fact was the man was an abuser all around. His own secretary feared him. He was not a well-liked man. Why be surprised that he was a tyrant on the home front too?

Judith didn't look at me, but I saw the large envelope on the desk, still sealed.

I nudged her, "You were right about Amir. He knew how to dig in the right places."

Judith lifted her head and a ghost of a smile appeared on her battered face. "You found something?"

"Yes, once you open that package, you can decide what you want to do with the information. Just know the evidence can influence the police to look into Edwin's business dealings further. There is enough there for the chief prosecuting attorney, which means things can spiral fast. I do have to warn you, Judith, it's going to be really bad. Neither Amir nor I can justify sitting on this information. There could be lives at stake."

Judith flashed a fearful look at me, then stared at the package, not seeming in a hurry to touch it. "I understand. Thank you both. I will make sure you both receive your final payments."

Hardly finished, I sighed. "I need to ask you something that pertains to the other part of your request last week."

Judith's eyes widened, "Go ahead."

"You asked me to destroy the photos. I know I did. Did you?"

Judith jerked her head as if I'd slapped her. "Yes, I shredded them the same night."

"You didn't create electronic copies, did you?"

Judith tried to frown but cringed instead. She held her hand to her temple. "No, of course not. Why are you asking?"

"Amir had copies. He said he retrieved them from one of the computers in this house."

Alarm crossed Judith's face. "What?"

"Someone took photos of the hard copies you had. Who would do that?"

Judith moved swiftly from around the desk with no warning and went out into the hallway.

I followed behind her. She ran up the wide staircase, holding onto the banister. "Janine? Janine."

Just the person I wanted to see. I traipsed up the stairs. When I reached the top of the stairs, Judith swung open a bedroom door and shouted, "Janine, answer me."

She stepped back out the room, swiveling her head from one side of the hall to the other as if she thought her daughter would appear. "Janine, where are you?"

Another bedroom door opened and Ethan stepped out. His jet black hair was spiked up in the back as if he'd been laying down. "Mom, why are you yelling?"

She rushed over to her son, "Where is your sister?"

"I don't know. She left the house."

Judith looked confused. "What? No, I saw her go upstairs."

The boy shrugged. "She left after you guys fought."

I raised an eyebrow. I climbed the rest of the stairs. "You and your daughter got into a fight? Is that where the bruise came from on your face?"

Judith held her head down. I looked over at Ethan. "Did your sister hit your mother?"

He stared back at me, his eyes fearful. "Who are you?"

"I'm a private investigator working for your mom. I need to talk to Janine. Where did she go?"

Judith shook her head. "You can go now, Ms. Manchester. I can handle this."

"No, you can't handle this. Where did Janine go? Why did your daughter do that to you? Is she violent?"

Ethan answered, "Janine was mad with me. She started hitting me and Mom stepped in and caught one of her fists to the face." He looked at his mother. "I'm sorry, Mom."

Judith's shoulders drooped. She rubbed her son's shoulder and brought him closer to her. "Janine has a temper. She's always had one since she was a little girl. A trait she apparently inherited from her dad."

Awareness dawned on me. "Has she run away before after a fight? Where could she have gone?"

Both Judith and Ethan shook their heads.

"Has Janine been in school? I heard she dropped out."

Judith whirled around and stared at me, "How did you know that?"

"I'm a private investigator, Judith. I have my ways. Why are you protecting her?"

Judith stepped away from her son and moved towards me. "No one knows that she left school. She's been having a difficult time. Once she's better, she will go back."

I sighed, "I'm guessing the police don't know that information. Who's this roommate and friend who confirmed Janine's alibi? Where has she been all this time, Judith?"

Ethan squealed, "She's been here at home."

Judith turned to her son, "That's enough, Ethan."

Realization hit me so hard, I clutched my stomach. "Judith, this is serious. Remember what I told you downstairs about the photos?"

Judith opened her mouth like a fish, but no sound came out.

"Where was Janine that night? Why would her friends lie for her?"

Ethan was looking back and forth between me and his mother. "What's she talking about, Mom?"

The only one in this house who seemed to be making sense was the thirteen year old, so I addressed my question to him. "The night you had your friends over, your mom made you all pizza, right?"

Ethan looked at his mom as if to get her approval.

Judith visibly trembled with her hands clenched.

I needed to get to the bottom of this. I wasn't going to put Judith in the same category as her husband, but I was starting to think this mother had her own secrets. I turned to Ethan, "Was your sister here?"

Ethan shook his head. "No, she went to see her friend."

Despite the fact I thought Judith was going to fly off the handle at any minute, I stepped closer. "What friend? Was she going to see Samantha?"

Ethan's voice dropped almost to a whisper. The boy could sense the tension coming from his mother. "I heard her talking on the phone with Samantha. She was going to move in with her, so she went to check out the room at the apartment."

Janine was there that night. Either Samantha gave her a key or she found one. "One more question. What was she driving?"

Ethan shrugged, "Her car."

Okay, that shot down one of my theories, but it gave a whole lot of ammunition to the theory dominating my mind. Without another word, I turned and sped back down the stairs. I thought I heard Judith calling my name behind me, but there was no time.

I knew who killed Samantha, I just wasn't quite sure why. But I had to find her to find out.

Chapter Thirty-One

Black Friday, 8:34 pm

"This is no time to be yelling at me, Moses." I shouted back into the phone. I knew contacting Moses for a second time in the same day was going to result in him tearing my head off. But I also knew I had to cover my behind. I might be a private investigator, but my credentials only took me so far. I needed real law enforcement.

Moses went silent. I knew he had to be counting to ten, which we both agreed one time never worked. He finally responded, "How did you manage to insert yourself into this investigation?"

I rolled my eyes. I was swiftly developing a headache. "Look, I'm trying to tell you that Janine Peters needs to be found and questioned. She was not at school. I don't know why her friends lied. I have a suspicion, if you question them again, either Janine or Judith asked them to lie."

"You're saying it was the daughter at Samantha's place?"

"It's a theory. Check her email. Janine asked Samantha if she could stay at her place. Her own

256

brother overheard her talking about going to live with Samantha. Samantha could have given her a key or Janine could have found a key. Cherry, the friend who had been staying at the apartment lost her bag. All of them were out at the same club that weekend. Instagram photos show them all together."

Moses sighed deeply into the phone.

"Look, she had two close friends. One of them is dead. I'm about to go see the other one."

"Amir?" Moses asked incredulously. "How do you know he didn't have anything to do with it? Maybe him and Janine were in on it together, and he gave her the key."

I didn't think about that. Still, my mind wouldn't go there. "No, I believe Amir learned a lot about Samantha in the days after her death. He wouldn't hurt her. If anything, Amir would protect Samantha. He always looked out for her."

"Whatever, Rena, you better not be walking into something."

"That's why I called you. You guys need to be looking for Janine. She's been having problems before she lost her best friend. She's hurt. Unstable. I don't know if she would harm anyone else, but she did get into a violent tussle with her little brother and her mother. Judith has a nasty bruise on her face." I slapped my steering wheel in frustration. "At this point, Janine could do more harm to herself. We just need to find her. Get her story."

"Okay. Keep in touch."

"Thanks, Moses." I hung up my Bluetooth and sat still in the Peters' driveway. I knew Moses and Baldwin would jump all over finding Janine.

But the photos was still bothering me.

Someone had taken pictures of the hard copies that Judith had. Probably with their phone. Then what? Did they send them anywhere?

I called Amir and brought him up to speed.

"I can't believe I didn't think about that before."

"About what?" I asked.

"Samantha told me that Janine dropped out of school. She didn't mention anything about her coming to live with her, but she said Janine had been having a rough time for a while. She had problems when she was in high school."

"Problems, like what kind of problems? Mental problems?"

"Yeah, she had these real awful mood swings. Like most people, I just thought she was just mean. But, Samantha was like, 'No, she's not mean,. She just doesn't feel well.'"

"Samantha knew her friend had some kind of mental illness. It's why she stayed friends with her when others wouldn't."

Amir let out a breath, "That was Sam for you. She would become friends with just about anybody. She had such a good heart."

"Amir, we have to find Janine. If she did something—"

"Why? Why would she do something to Sam? I mean she was messed up, but I believe Janine loved Sam like a sister."

"Suppose she wasn't in her right mind, Amir?"

He was quiet for a moment. "Rena, I have something I need to tell you."

I sat up in my car seat, "What?"

"Remember at my house yesterday, the person who triggered the alarm?"

"Yes, you know who it was?"

"I'm pretty sure it was Janine."

I thought for a moment back to the tall, slim figure. "Amir, why didn't you say something?"

"I wasn't sure until I looked back at the footage."

"Didn't you shoot a round off from your gun?"

"Yeah, I didn't hit her. Plus, I didn't know who it was when I was running around the house last night."

I frowned, "Amir, why would she hang around your house?"

"I don't know. She'd been calling all day and I haven't been taking her calls. Maybe she thought she'd just drop by the house."

"She's in trouble. I know she's not your friend, but she was Samantha's friend. We have to find her to know what really happened that night."

"What do you want me to do, Rena?"

"Where do you think she would go if she saw those photos?"

Amir was silent like he was thinking. Then his deep voice broke through the line confirming my own thoughts. "She probably went to see her dad."

"Shall we take a trip to Pawleys Island?"

Chapter Thirty-Two

Black Friday - 9:02 pm

I picked up Amir and we headed off down Highway 17. I was going on one of my hunches. Moses threw another fit on the phone, when he should have been grateful that I was sharing the journey along the way. I had my SIG in a holster, just in case. It was the first time I ever thought I might need it.

I pray I don't have to use it.

Amir looked at me from the passenger seat, "We packing tonight?" His eye was on the holster which was not hidden very well under my jacket.

"Never know what to expect. I usually keep this in the glove of my car."

Amir nodded. "Do you know if Judith opened the package?"

"She was a bit preoccupied with her daughter. Did you send a package anywhere else?"

"Quite a few places. The solicitor's office should find a package in the morning. I have good information that the chief prosecuting attorney has been wanting to get his hands on Edwin for years."

"Smart man." I glanced at Amir. "You're not going to start any trouble tonight, right, if we see Edwin?"

He smirked, "No. I'd like to see the man get what he's owed, but I don't have to be the one to do it. "

We arrived near the Peters' home. Only two weeks ago, I'd staked this same place out, taking photos of a young woman whose life was in the hands of Edwin Peters. The lights were ablaze in the home just like that night.

I drove past, catching sight of a Nissan Murano haphazardly parked on the grass. "Is that Janine's car?"

Amir looked back, "Yeah. This can't be good."

"I know." I drove down the road and made a U-turn. My maneuvering of the car brought a deja vu feeling along with it. I even parked in the same spot and cut the engine. I still had Moses' shouts of warning in my head. "How do you want to do this?"

"We can always ring the doorbell. You can say you were looking for her."

I nodded, "I could say her mother was worried about her."

"Sounds good to me." Amir reached for the door.

"Wait." I reached for his arm. "We got to make sure this is the right thing to do."

He stared at me. "Rena, you drove here. What did you want to happen?"

I sighed deeply. "Are you sure about this?"

"Look, if you worried about me doing something stupid, I will stay out of the way. I'm not letting you go in there by yourself though. You need backup."

I couldn't argue with that, so I let go of his hand and climbed out the other side of my car.

Instead of walking straight up to the door, I took the same path I did on my previous venture at the house. Amir followed me.

He whispered, "What are you doing?"

Going back to the scene of a crime. I didn't want to say that out loud. "I just want an idea of what we could be walking into."

We snuck around the shrubbery of the house. The smell of the ocean was strong, but the wind was not as vicious tonight. Though I could hear the crashing waves, there was almost a strange calmness. I squatted down in the same spot I took photos a few weeks ago. Amir squatted next to me.

He whispered, "You can see everything from back here."

I nodded, peering into the window. What caught my attention was Edwin first. The man appeared visibly upset. He was talking to someone in front of him, waving his hands as if he was trying to calm the person.

I moved slightly to the right knowing the person Edwin was talking to had to be his own daughter.

What I didn't expect was to see Janine with bloodshot eyes.

Holding a gun.

I sucked in a breath.

Amir grabbed my arm, "What?"

I swallowed, "Janine is holding her dad at gunpoint."

Now what do we do?

There was no time to ponder that question. Edwin Peters fell back clutching his chest.

Chapter Thirty-Three

Black Friday - 9:11 pm

I turned to Amir, "Remember how we said we were going to ring the doorbell?"

"Yeah."

"That's what we're going to do."

He pulled me back down. "Are you sure about this? Maybe we should wait for backup."

"No, I'm not completely sure, but Janine just shot her dad. Call 9-1-1."

Amir blew out a breath. "Okay." He whipped out his phone as we sprinted around the house. I rang the doorbell, and then pulled my coat over my chest. I wanted to make sure my holster wasn't obvious.

No one came to the door, so I rang the doorbell again.

Janine's pale face showed at the window almost giving me a heart attack. She looked at us, but her eyes locked on Amir's face. A few seconds later, she opened the door. I noticed her arm was behind her back.

"Amir." She looked at him, "What are you doing here?"

Amir looked at me for direction, so I spoke first. "Your mother was worried about you. She wanted us to see if you were okay."

Janine barely glanced at me. Her eyes were so focused on Amir, I knew he had to be uncomfortable. To break the eye contact going on, I stepped towards the door, "Is your father here? We need to speak to him."

Janine frowned, "Why do you need to talk to him?"

Amir spoke, "I'd like to talk to you, while Ms. Manchester talks to your father. I know it's been awhile. Can we come in?"

Janine flinched. "Wait a moment." She shut the door back.

I looked at Amir. "She seems rather obsessed with you."

He nodded, "She has been for a while."

I tilted my head. "You hadn't mentioned this before."

"Because I was trying to avoid…"

The door was snatched open again. Amir nudged me to go in first. I stepped by Janine, who once again had her eyes locked on Amir in the creepiest stare I'd ever seen.

When I entered the house, the majestic hallway would have normally taken my breath away but it wasn't the time or place to get caught up in the architecture.

"Where's your father?"

"He's in the kitchen. You can join him, if you'd like."

"Okay." I looked back at Amir, he didn't look as calm and cool as he usually did. In fact, I would have to say, he was staring at Janine like he was little afraid of her.

I walked back towards where I thought the kitchen was located. The large home had an open concept where you could see most of the house from the center. I ventured back towards a kitchen that gleamed and sparkled as if the appliances were brand new. The large windows facing the ocean reflected the home's interior on the inside.

I didn't see or hear any signs of Edwin. "Mr. Peters, are you here?" I stopped when I reached the giant island in the middle of the kitchen. My nose twitched. A distinct coppery odor permeated the air, and it smelled as if a gun was recently shot. I rushed around the island to find Edwin Peters lying on the floor.

She really had shot her dad. I went over to Edwin, who was clutching his chest, now covered with blood. "Hold on, help is on the way."

His eyes rolled in my direction, but they weren't focused. He was fading fast. I walked from behind the island. Janine was moving towards me, pointing her gun at me.

"You shouldn't be here."

I held up my hands, wondering if I should reach for my own gun.

Amir was behind her. "Janine, stop." He threw himself in front of me to ward off Janine from coming any closer.

Janine waved the gun, shooting wildly.

When Amir went down, I screamed.

Chapter Thirty-Four

Black Friday - 9:59 pm

Not today, Lord. I did not want having killed someone on my conscience, but I reached for my SIG with no hesitation. I pointed it towards Janine.

"What are you doing? Put the gun down, Janine. You shot your dad and now Amir."

I glanced over at Amir. He moaned. From what I could tell it looked like the bullet hit in the lower abdomen. The blood soaking his shirt was making me nervous.

I glanced at Edwin before directing my attention back to Janine. His body lay still, not making a single movement.

"Hold on, Amir. Help is coming."

I prayed Moses and Baldwin were on their way or had made contact with the Pawleys Island police.

Janine still held the gun, though now it was pointing to the floor.

I kept mine aimed at Janine's head. All my training at the gun range, I still wasn't sure I was prepared for this. I could not shoot to kill, but I wasn't about to let this crazy woman shoot me too.

She swayed as if her feet were unsteady and any moment she would fall over. "Amir, I'm sorry. I love you, you know that."

You got a funny way of showing how much you love people, I thought, but I wouldn't dare say that out loud.

Janine looked over at me as if she remembered I was there.

Silence hung between us. She stared at me and I stared back at her. My eyes went to her hand that gripped the gun. She was trembling like she was coming down off something.

"Janine, please, put the gun down so we can get Amir some help. If you love him, don't let him die."

"I didn't mean to hurt him," she cried. "He shouldn't have jumped in front of you."

"I know, Janine. It's okay. Let's get Amir some help and you can get some help too."

"No. I did this. I should be punished. I didn't meant to hurt her either."

I sucked in a breath. My hands were starting to tremble. I made myself stay alert. "You didn't mean to hurt Samantha either. You loved her. You wanted to move in with her."

She swung the gun towards me. "Don't talk about her. She..."

"She what?"

"I heard her on the phone. She was asking my dad for money. I heard Mom say one time that Samantha was just around me for my money." Janine scoffed, "Most people were around me for money. I thought she was my true friend. I didn't know she was asking my dad for money."

Janine stared off beyond me. Her mind had zoned in on a thought that made her brows move inward. Something that I could only describe as a chill snaked up my back. The girl's face contorted with a venomous rage, and her voice was wooden, "She wanted a lot more than money from my dad. The skank!"

The photos. There was no doubt in my mind that she was referring to the very same photos I took here at this house. After this was all over, and I was praying I would survive this, I had a feeling it would be a long time before I ever took on a cheating spouse case.

I wanted to reign Janine back in. Her being angry and holding a gun had not worked out too well for the men on the floor. Amir still moved, his moans were actually positive.

"So you argued with her? She came home that night and you had a key to her apartment."

Janine frowned. "I was staying at her apartment. She let me stay there after the other girl left. I thought she was going to get some food, but I heard her on the phone with my dad. He was mad with me because I left school. He told me he was going to disown me, yet he could give my friend money." She spat.

I sucked in my breath trying to will myself to breathe. Janine was absently waving the gun, while I held mine steady. Waiting and praying I didn't have to use it. "You didn't mean to kill her. She fell."

Janine's face cringed and her eyes watered. "I hit her. She didn't hit back. I hit her again and again. Then I pushed her. She fell and knocked her head hard against the stove, but the way she slid down, her neck looked funny. She had marks around her neck. I didn't know where those came from, but she wouldn't wake up. I shook her and she didn't move."

"So you left her?"

"I went home. Mother wouldn't turn me out."

I forced myself to ask, "Did you tell your mother what you did?"

Janine wiped her face with one hand, but still she held the gun. "I told her I had a fight with Sam. Mother said everything would be fine in the morning. Friends fight."

We stood in silence.

Everything wasn't fine in the morning.

I held my gun steadier, "Don't do this. Put the gun down or you will make it worse for yourself."

She mouthed, "I'm sorry." She raised her gun.

But I squeezed the trigger. Janine jerked backwards as her gun went off. I threw myself to the floor feeling the bullet whiz by my face. Though my face was stinging I kept my eyes on her. Waiting. My hands still gripped the gun like it had become a part of my hand.

Janine screamed and writhed on the floor. The gun was no longer in her hand.

I jumped up and kicked her gun away, keeping mine on her.

My shot had entered Janine's shoulder. She held her shoulder as blood streamed through her fingers. I could hear sirens now. Maybe I'd heard them before but blocked them out when I saw Janine swing her gun towards me.

Cops were shouting outside the door. I slowly stepped back and put my weapon down on the ground. Right as cops burst through the door, I held up my arms. I wasn't trying to die tonight from cops either.

Chapter Thirty-Five

Saturday, November 24 - 2:30 pm

Moses and Baldwin showed up on the scene. This wasn't their jurisdiction, but they waited as I gave the Pawleys Island deputy my statement. Thanks to Moses, the cop let me go. Instead of going home to take a shower, I went to the hospital.

Both Amir and Janine had been taken into surgery.

Edwin Peters didn't make it. I briefly saw Judith with her son behind her. I wasn't sure how to feel about the Peters' circumstances. Some of what Edwin did still needed to come to light though he would no longer be the one to stand trial. Still, there were others who needed to take some responsibility. That would all fall on the solicitor's office.

My phone chirped with phone calls and texts. One from Clay and Bev. Even Mama called. I explained I was alright, even though I had a slight scratch on my cheek. There was no way I wanted to tell anyone about the bullet that grazed my face. I'd keep that to myself.

Moses finally showed up and told me to go home. I did, but I returned a few hours later.

I stayed by Amir's side until he opened his eyes. I knew no one else would come. He didn't have family. Though I had some doubts about him along the way, I felt like he needed someone there. Plus, the man saved my life. That bullet was meant for me.

When he opened his eyes. I smiled. "Hey, gorgeous."

He grinned back. "I have never hurt this bad before."

"Well, I've heard getting shot is an experience."

He chuckled, then winced. "Is she okay?"

"Janine? She's out of surgery. I think she going to be taken for a psych evaluation. I have a feeling she will be on suicide watch for a while too."

"I can't believe she did it. They were best friends. Samantha loved her like a sister."

"I'm sure Janine did too, but she had mental issues. I honestly believe she didn't mean to kill her, she pushed her too hard. I think Judith knew her daughter went over the edge. She's been unstable a long time."

Amir frowned, "Janine has always been the life of the party. Partied hard. There was so many times when Samantha would call me to help get Janine home. Most of the time she would end up crashing at Samantha's place."

"So she had a key?"

"Yeah."

I swallowed. "I wish I'd convinced Samantha to let me in the apartment that night. She stepped out and closed the door. I didn't think anything about it, but Janine was already in there. Simmering with anger, ready for a confrontation."

Amir reached for my hand. "There's nothing you could have done. She reached out to me and I didn't go see her. I should have stopped by too."

I didn't remove my hand from Amir's because I suspected this all hit him a lot harder than me. He'd known Samantha as his little sister and he was her protector.

I sat with him for a long time until I saw the pain medicine had him back sleep again. I left, knowing I would return to check on him.

I'd arrived home long enough to feed Callie before the doorbell rang.

I peeked out the door and stepped back. It wasn't like I could run and hide.

Trey.

I ushered Trey inside without saying a word. I really didn't know what to say. It was good to see him. He'd never looked better dressed down in a USC sweatshirt, blue jeans and sneakers. Of course, he smelled good. He reached out and placed his hands on my shoulders. The gesture made me want to cry. In fact, that's exactly what I did, blubbered like a baby.

What was wrong with me?

"I heard you had a rough night," he said softly.

"Got into a gun fight. I guess Queen was right about my profession being all dangerous." I said in between sniffles.

Trey gripped my arms and guided me to the couch. "Moses said you handled the situation as good as any cop would."

I wiped my eyes, but the tears kept coming. "Moses said that? All I heard from him was how crazy I was for going there."

Trey chuckled. "He had a few choice words about that too. Not very godly words. Still he's proud of you. You saved that girl from herself."

I swallowed. Silence enveloped the room as I sat on the couch with Trey's arms wrapped around me.

"You got justice for Samantha. It's time for you to rest."

"I'm going to try, but I still have work to do. More justice to pursue."

Trey stiffened. "How's Amir?"

I eyed him. "I'm surprised you're asking about him."

"He saved your life, Rena."

I nodded. "He will heal. Did you know Amir is young enough to be my son?"

Trey grinned. "So. Don't women your age like to experience being a cougar?"

"A cougar? Really?" I grabbed a pillow off the couch and flung it at him. He caught the pillow.

I sighed and fell back on the couch. "In all seriousness, I have come a long way from where I used to be. But I know there's more work God has to do in me. I grew up with people judging me, and it kept me away from God. I don't want anything or anyone to mess with my relationship."

He grinned. "None of us have reached the finished line, and we all have room for improvement. The fact is you're a strong woman who has come through some mighty crazy situations. I mean you're living the dream job despite your injuries a few years ago. God has your back, and so do I. Don't forget that."

"Thanks. I won't forget."

He looked at me. Really looked at me. "I'm proud of you. If I act a little crazy sometimes, it's because I love you, Serena Manchester."

I stared into his eyes. "I love you too, Trey Evans. Always have. I'm still scared of this."

He put his arm around me. "I am too, but I'm not going to lose you this time. There's nothing you can do to push me away."

I snuggled up next to Trey, not caring that I'd been trying to avoid him. That all seemed silly now. God let me live through one more event where death was at my door.

I was grateful for yet another chance.

Other Books

SERENA MANCHESTER SERIES
Hostile Eyewitness
Bittersweet Motives

REED FAMILY SERIES
Broken Heart
Troubled Heart
Relentless Heart

VICTORY GOSPEL SERIES
When Rain Falls
When Memories Fade
When Perfection Fails

EUGEENA PATTERSON MYSTERIES
Deep Fried Trouble
Oven Baked Secrets
Lemon Filled Disaster

About the Author

Tyora Moody is the author of Soul-Searching Suspense books which include the *Reed Family Series*, *Eugeena Patterson Mysteries*, *Serena Manchester Series*, and the *Victory Gospel Series*. When Tyora isn't working for a client or doing something literary, she enjoys reading, spending time with family, binge-watching crime shows, catching a movie on the big screen, and traveling.

To contact Tyora about book club discussions, visit her online at **TyoraMoody.com**. You can also find her online on Facebook, Instagram and Twitter.

COMING SPRING 2020

Dangerous Confessions

Serena Manchester Series, Book #3
TYORA MOODY

Chapter One

Myrtle Beach, South Carolina

Friday, January 3, 9:43 pm

I was past ready for something to go down. Anything.

My phone chirped for the third time. I didn't even bother to look at it this time. I knew it was Trey. We'd argued before I left town this morning. My long-time friend and current love interest claimed he supported me. But it was becoming obvious to me that my choice of profession as a private investigator got under his skin. He was a minister with a very prominent standing in our community. My cases often brought eyebrow raising, deep sighing and extended lectures on how I endangered my life.

I have always had this driving force to expose the truth. Unfortunately, revealing someone else's ugliness can backfire. I'd managed to find myself in life-threatening situations more times than I liked to admit. Still I knew without a doubt God's purpose for me was to do exactly what I was doing. Somebody had to be an advocate for victims of injustices. Thanks to my newly formed relationship with God, these days I sought justice with a lot more scruples than I had as a reporter in my past life.

I sighed deeply and lifted the glass of soda water to my lips. I'd been sitting at the bar for about forty minutes now. Earlier this week, I had conversations with the bartender and the waitress currently on the clock. Both told me what I needed to know.

So, I continued to wait. In my earpiece, I heard the tired voice of my young associate Amir Wright. "Do you think this is the right night?"

I smiled. Amir was young, but definitely had skills. I wouldn't have ever considered tonight's stakeout without him as backup. Something that Trey didn't like either. I turned away from a trio of young women who'd appeared at the bar. They were dressed for a night out on the town, all adorning black dresses and stilettos. I pulled out my phone, pretending to talk. I spoke softly. "I'm wondering the same. I haven't seen any of the subjects yet."

Amir countered, "Didn't both the bartender and the waitress mention first Fridays of the month? Maybe they meet up later than we suspected."

The group of women's chatter was too much in my ear, so I walked away from the bar, headed towards the lobby. "It's almost ten o'clock. You think you can make it another hour?"

"Hey, I'm all in with you."

On our first case together only a few months ago, Amir had been shot, on Black Friday, of all days. While he was back in the swing of things, I knew sitting around in a hotel room with the surveillance equipment was probably not good for his body. Then again, the man owned a cybersecurity company. He was in his element, and I knew he wouldn't have it any other way.

I scolded softly, "You really shouldn't being doing this. Let's wrap this up so you can get some rest. Plus, you know this old lady can't hang too long."

Amir chuckled, "Past your bedtime, huh?"

"Not really. I'm definitely disappointed though." Especially after I did my homework and prepared for this night for weeks, even through the holidays. It didn't help that I was feeling slightly guilty about my argument with Trey. I really needed to return to my room and call him back. Never let the sun go down on your anger. That was something we both agreed to do.

The hotel was buzzing with activity, people arriving bedraggled from traveling or heading out for the local nightlife. I looked up to see a woman dressed in a fuchsia pants suit walking in my direction. Our eyes connected and I immediately had the sense I'd seen her before. She was tall, thin like a super model, except this woman wasn't a young thing. Her bobbed hair was almost a white blond. She'd loosened her orange scarf so that it hung down, exposing a scrawny neck.

When she looked at me, recognition reflected in her eyes.

I heard an audible gasp from her and was surprised to see her stop in the middle of the lobby. Curious about who she was and how she knew me, I paused mid-stride and faced her.

When the woman spoke, her Southern drawl came out deep and throaty. "Serena Manchester?"

I raised an eyebrow, because it was when she spoke that the cobwebs in my mind started to glide away. I knew this woman a long time ago, back during my crime reporting days in Charlotte. She was a major part of one my most popular stories.

I inquired, "Deena? Deena Huffman?"

Deena's smile wasn't warm and inviting, more like the kind you gave your worst enemy. Her gesture was meant to be polite, but she was not happy to see me. "You remember me?"

I nodded, "How could I not? You moved out the spotlight after the trial. Have you been here in Myrtle Beach all this time?"

Her eyes shifted behind me. "I've been a lot of places, but I do have a beach home here that belonged to my … husband."

"Your deceased husband." The one who she in fact was accused of killing.

Her eyes flashed as if she read my mind. "I was acquitted you know."

I couldn't wipe the smirk off my face. "I'm well aware. I sat in the courtroom everyday covering the trial."

Her lips thinned. "You were also the one to break the story for the police."

"I'd been following your husband for over a year. Brent Huffman was quite the character. If I remember, money laundering was his thing along with a heroin addiction."

Deena's eyes were cold. "I don't miss him. He wasn't a good husband." Her eyes shifted behind me again as though she was watching for someone. "He wasn't a good man at all. I'm sorry he died the way he did."

I narrowed my eyes, "Which you still claim to know nothing about?"

Her eyes flickered on my face. "I didn't kill him. But I have my suspicions."

Interesting. "Did you ever share them with the police?"

"No." She shook her head and dropped her voice, "I'm not crazy. I love my life."

I frowned at this unexpected revelation. Deena was scared of her husband's true killer. But she stood trial for his murder. Why?

Deena openly eyed something or someone behind me, her eyes had widened. Her nervousness rubbed off on me.

Why was she really here? This impromptu meeting didn't seem like a coincidence. I turned my head slightly to observe three suited men walk into the lobby. They each had a young beautiful woman on their arms.

Too young. In fact, these were the same women who were sitting at the bar a few minutes ago. *Were they escorts of some sort?*

My skin prickled as thoughts of my last case loomed. A young woman had been murdered. As I studied her life, I'd found some unsavory elements that lead me here tonight. I was pretty sure the men that arrived were in the center of my investigation.

And Deena seemed to recognize them. Her stance was still as she clutched her large designer purse in front of her.

Before I could ask her anything, Deena spoke, her words rushed. "It was good to see you again. I have to go." She took off behind the men, all heading towards the elevators.

I held my phone up to my ear, "Amir, you still there?"

"Yeah, what was all that about? You ran into someone you knew?"

"I did, but we can talk about her later." I took in a sharp intake of breath as I scoped out the men in suits. "Right now, all of the men are here. I'm going to follow."

Amir responded, his stressed tone reminding me of Trey's earnest pleas earlier. "Rena, be careful."

"Don't worry, Amir. I got this."

If Deena Huffman was associated with these men, I knew we were in for a night of revelations. Her fear should have made me pause. Instead, I headed towards the elevators too, praying that Trey's worst fears about my job would not come to light.